WHERE IS SEAN GOING?

I went back to the window. What I saw bugged me out.

Sean was half asleep and standing wobbly like he was about to fall over. His mother put one hand under his arm to hold him up. She had a small suitcase in her other hand. Tiny enough for a weekend trip. I backed a bit out of the window so they wouldn't see me.

What's up with that? Sean had told me he would be around this weekend on punishment. Why were they leaving? Did they have a family emergency?

"Come on, Sean," Jackie said. She took him by the hand and led him off the court. They disappeared behind a building.

I wanted to wake up Kyle and tell him what I had just seen, but all these thoughts were going through my head. Did Sean know he was bouncing this weekend? Yes or no? He never went somewhere without telling me first. Where were they going at so early in the morning? With a suitcase?

I let Kyle sleep and decided not to tell him what I had just seen. Maybe because I didn't want to hear Kyle say something like, "We should mind our own business." I wasn't in the mood to hear that, because I was worried about Sean. He didn't look like he knew where his mom was taking him. Was she taking him somewhere to leave him?

OTHER BOOKS YOU MAY ENJOY

Torrey
Maldonado

SECRET
SATURDAYS

SPEAK

Published by the Penguin Group

Penguin Group (USA) Inc., 345 Hudson Street, New York, New York 10014, U.S.A.

Penguin Group (Canada), 90 Eglinton Avenue East, Suite 700, Toronto, Ontario, Canada M4P 2Y3
(a division of Pearson Penguin Canada Inc.)

Penguin Books Ltd, 80 Strand, London WC2R 0RL, England

Penguin Ireland, 25 St Stephen's Green, Dublin 2, Ireland (a division of Penguin Books Ltd)

Penguin Group (Australia), 250 Camberwell Road, Camberwell, Victoria 3124, Australia
(a division of Pearson Australia Group Pty Ltd)

Penguin Books India Pvt Ltd, 11 Community Centre,
Panchsheel Park, New Delhi - 110 017, India

Penguin Group (NZ), 67 Apollo Drive, Auckland 0632, New Zealand
(a division of Pearson New Zealand Ltd.)

Penguin Books (South Africa) (Pty) Ltd, 24 Sturdee Avenue,
Rosebank, Johannesburg 2196, South Africa

Registered Offices: Penguin Books Ltd, 80 Strand, London WC2R 0RL, England

First published in the United States of America by G. P. Putnam's Sons,
a division of Penguin Young Readers Group, 2010
Published by Speak, an imprint of Penguin Group (USA) Inc., 2012

7 9 10 8

THE LIBRARY OF CONGRESS HAS CATALOGED THE G. P. PUTNAM'S SONS EDITION AS FOLLOWS:
Maldonado, Torrey.
Secret Saturdays / Torrey Maldonado.
p. cm.
Summary: Twelve-year-old boys living in a rough part of New York confront questions about
what it means to be a friend, a father, and a man.
ISBN: 978-0-399-25158-0 (hc)
[1. Inner cities—Fiction. 2. Single-parent families—Fiction. 3. Interpersonal relations—Fiction.
4. Racially mixed people—Fiction. 5. African Americans—Fiction. 6. Schools—Fiction.
7. Brooklyn (New York, N.Y.)—Fiction.]
I. Title.
PZ7.M2927Se 2010
[Fic]—dc22 2009010361

Speak ISBN 978-0-14-241747-8

Text set in Chaparral Pro

Printed in the United States of America

For my mother, Carmen.
Without you, I wouldn't be who I am

Sean

"SON! YOUR EARS ARE BIGGER THAN BASEBALL GLOVES."

Manny was a known troublemaker but I still couldn't believe he was trying to clown Sean.

Out here the rule was "Dis or get dissed on." The best disser was king of the hill. That was Sean. You became the new king by knocking down the old king. I guess that's why out of all the tables in our school cafeteria, Manny came to ours.

Manny was a husky Dominican kid who looked white. Italian or something. He had green crossed eyes, a thick neck, and he always kept the same pissed face on. He had no sense and messed with anybody.

"You speaking to me?" Sean said.

"Yeah, you, elephant ears." Manny laughed. He

probably thought he was hard because he had two seventh graders with him. He looked like he was trying to dress hard too. The end of September is chilly, even in our lunchroom. But Manny kept his button-up shirt wide open. His white tank top showed.

Sean eyed him up and down. "You rocking clothes from a ninety-nine-cents store and you trying to dis me?"

The two seventh graders who had come over with Manny laughed, then gave Sean a pound.

"What up, Panchi," Sean said. "What up, Rob." He made room for them to sit.

Manny's eyes bugged out. He probably thought they just sort of knew Sean, not that they were so cool. Manny was standing all alone now.

If someone clowned Sean, he didn't just dis back enough to shut the kid up. He took it to a whole other level. So I knew Sean wasn't about to let Manny off the hook so easy.

Sean winked at me, Kyle, and Vanessa, and we understood what his wink meant. We had known Sean since fourth grade, and his favorite boxer—a Heavyweight Champion of the World—winked that way before he threw his one-two knockout combo.

"Everybody here knows your family lives in a homeless shelter," Sean told Manny. He waved at his sandwich in front of him. "Here. I only took two bites from my hero. Take my leftovers to your family." Sean pulled a dollar out of his pocket. "And this is so you don't have to beg on the train later."

Kids at the table busted out laughing. Me, Kyle, and Vanessa did too.

Manny opened his mouth to say something back to Sean, then closed it. His eyes were hurt looking and his face turned red.

"Yoo-hoo," Sean said, waving at Manny. "Hello? You too hurt to say something?" Sean tapped Panchi's forearm. "Get your man Manny a Kleenex."

"He's not my man anymore," Panchi said, and sucked his teeth at Manny. "Punk."

Manny got mad, tightened his hands into fists, and took a step toward Sean but stopped when he saw Ms. Feeney, our Advisory teacher, coming over.

"Everything okay over here?" she asked.

Everyone nodded yes at the same time, except Manny.

Manny looked at Ms. Feeney, at us, and then he bounced. After Ms. Feeney watched Manny leave, she nodded at Sean the way police who patrolled my neighborhood said hi to teenage guys who chilled on benches. There was something mean about it. Another teacher called Ms. Feeney away before she could say something to us.

Dissing is like boxing. There's a winner and a

loser. Winners leave smiling. Losers end up sorry looking and deflated like a popped balloon.

To dis someone, you need to find something wrong with them. Nothing was wrong with Sean, except his ears poked out a little.

Almost nobody had nicer gear than him. He always had brand-new kicks, a hot cell phone, and iPods.

His schoolwork was like his clothes. He was competitive. His assignments were super-neat, on time, all the time, and he got good grades.

He had a nice father and mother. They loved him.

And he was mad popular. Girls stayed stalking him. Sean was half Black and half Puerto Rican, like me, and girls thought he was cute because he looked like the rapper T.I. but in the sixth grade. He had T.I.'s same shape face, light brown skin, eyes, and haircut. In fifth grade, some girls even called Sean "Little T.I." for months. Back when they did that, me and Kyle teased Sean in girly voices and said, "Hey, Little T.I." He'd snap back, "Justin, that's why you a mini Nas and Kyle you a Souljah Boy with glasses."

Right now, Sean put his fist out to Kyle for a pound. "I got that one."

Kyle gave Sean his props. "You got it."

Sean reached over to Vanessa. "Gimme mine."

She said flirty, "You got it," and gave him a pound.

Sean stretched his arm over to me and held his fist up for a pound. Sean was The Man.

"You got that one," I said, punching my fist against his.

Sean's Not a Fighter

"WHO THIS BIGHEAD?" Sean nodded at the Latino guy standing next to Ms. Feeney.

"Probably Ms. Feeney's boyfriend," I joked. I was used to Sean saying some things, but him calling people "bigheads" was new. I wondered where he got it from.

Ms. Feeney was our only Black teacher. She had dreadlocks to her shoulders and almost a white girl's accent. We had her Advisory class only once a week. Fridays, eighth period. Our last class of the day.

"Everyone," Ms. Feeney began, "this is Juan Jones. He is a former gang member. He'll explain how his neighborhood and school pushed him to join a gang. I want you to listen."

"You can call me Jay," the gang guy said. He folded his arms and stepped into the middle of the circle. He dressed like he was going to work or church. Crisp white collared shirt. Slacks. Nice shoes. His small Afro was shaped up neat. He was maybe Puerto Rican or Dominican. Only one thing about him said he once was in a gang. His tats. He had a tear-shaped tattoo under his left eye. His right hand had tattooed letters on the back between his thumb and index finger. Everyone was listening.

"Family," Jay said. "It starts with family. Where I'm from, a normal family ain't normal. I grew up without a pops. That was normal because most kids in my projects didn't have dads. Raise your hand if you grew up without a father."

I looked around to see who would raise their hand.

Shaquan sat two seats from me. His dad was a drug dealer who had gotten shot and killed. Shaquan didn't have a father. He didn't raise his hand.

Becky was maybe four seats from me. She came from a crazy family. Her pops smoked crack, lived in the streets, and had no teeth in his mouth. Plus, Becky's sisters and brothers were in foster care. Becky didn't raise her hand.

Sean was right next to me. Even though his dad took care of him and his moms, his dad hadn't lived with him for the past two years. Sean didn't raise his hand.

My father was ghost too.

A few years back, he bounced on me and my mother after she found out he was cheating on her. He moved down south, and we haven't heard from him since. I'm half glad he left. But sometimes when I see other kids with their dads, I feel like, "Why don't I have that?" Plus, since he broke out, we had to go on welfare because of Ma's bad leg. She hurt it the year before my pops left when we picnicked in Sunset Park. She fell while trying to Rollerblade and her leg broke in a few places.

When he lived with us, my father was like a lot of men out here. They posed on every corner and pretended to be all hard and important. All fronts and good for nothing. Some of them even lived off allowances their grown sons and daughters gave them. They were just supersized boys.

I don't blame Shaquan, Becky, or Sean. I wasn't raising my hand to talk about my father either. Why put it on blast that your dad wasn't around? Kids will just make fun of that later.

Jay made a face like he didn't believe all our dads lived with us. "Anyway," he said, "my pops had parts of him that me and my brothers and sisters didn't know about."

I leaned over and whispered to Sean, "This guy is corny."

Sean nodded real slow like he was saying, "Yep!"

"Sean, if you got something to say, say it out loud," Manny said, starting trouble again like he did in the lunchroom. "Ms. Feeney, Sean's whispering because he's too scared to raise his hand and say he don't have a father." Manny turned back to Sean. "Raise your hand."

Some kids laughed at that.

"Manny," Ms. Feeney said, and shot him a mean look. She stepped into the circle next to the Latino guy. She looked embarrassed. She raised her hand and made her peace sign. That was her way to get us quiet without yelling. "Sorry," she told Jay.

"It's cool," Jay said.

As soon as kids stopped laughing, Sean said, "Manny, at least I don't have a lazy eye. One of your eyes looks left and the other stares right. I could stand right in front of your nose and you wouldn't even see me."

"Sean." Ms. Feeney frowned at him and shook her head "No." She did her V sign again, but the class stayed noisy.

"Shut up!" Manny shouted at the kids laughing at him. He stood up like he could make us listen to him, but we laughed harder.

Jay, the gang guy, smiled at Ms. Feeney. "It's okay. Kids will be kids, right?"

She gave the class such a dirty look that one by one we got quiet. When the class got completely silent, she apologized to Jay again and said, "Please continue." Then she told us, "Sit straight and act mature."

We fixed ourselves in our seats and Jay started speaking again, but Sean cut him off. "Manny," Sean said. "At least, I used to live with my father. Before he moved to Puerto Rico. Do you even know who your real father is?"

The whole class exploded. This time, Ms. Feeney tried to get control by staring hard at us, but everyone just laughed louder.

Manny jumped up like he wanted to fight Sean. Ms. Feeney got in front of Manny fast and put her hand on his chest. "Go in the hallway," she said. She told Sean he had detention, and to the rest of the class she said, "What happened here tells me this class isn't ready for today's guest speaker, so I'm canceling today's Advisory. Take out your independent reading books from your literacy class. Everyone will read quietly for the rest of the period."

About half the class sucked their teeth, rolled their eyes, and moaned.

"All because of stupid Manny," a girl's voice said.

"God!" some boy breathed out real heavy.

"I didn't want to hear this man anyway," another kid went.

Everyone was heated, but we all slowly pulled our books from our backpacks. As I sat up, Ms. Feeney told Jay loud enough for the class to hear, "I apologize. It's unfortunate this class loses its opportunity to hear you speak."

He smiled. "I'll still speak with them if you want."

Ms. Feeney said, "No, no. This class doesn't deserve you." She eyed everyone. I opened my book fast and pretended to read.

When Advisory ended, me and Sean grabbed our book bags to bounce, but Ms. Feeney rolled up on us with the quickness and told us to stay in our seats.

"Is this the second time today I saw you make a kid want to fight you?" she asked Sean.

Sean shrugged. "I don't know."

"Am I in trouble too?" I asked her, wondering why she'd make me stay.

"Justin, you're okay," she said. "You don't have to wait for Sean if you don't want to."

"I'll stay," I said. I did want to see what would happen to Sean. He was my best friend.

Ms. Feeney asked him, "So someone insults you

and you turn it into a competition. Put him down harder and tell everybody listening the ugliest truth about him?"

"He talked about my father," Sean said out the side of his mouth. "So I talked about his. We even."

"Did that bother you? When he talked about your dad?"

"No. Why would it bother me? I have a father. Right, Justin?"

"Yeah," I said. "He just lives in Puerto Rico."

"Exactly," Sean said.

That was true.

When me, Sean, Kyle, and Vanessa became cool in fourth grade, Sean told us his pops moved to PR to take care of their family's house there and run their parents' farm. Sean's mother and father stayed together and him and his dad kept tight because Sean's dresser drawer always had stuff his pops sent him from PR. Puerto Rican toys, key chains, and stuff. How? His moms was a cashier at IKEA. That money came from his pops.

"I know you have a father," Ms. Feeney said. "And I also know you really liked hurting Manny just because. Lately, you seem to enjoy being nasty to kids. But why, Sean? It'll only make kids want to fight you, and you're not a fighter."

"Mmm," Sean hummed like he was saying, "Whatever you say." He rolled his eyes and stared at the ceiling.

But Ms. Feeney was 100 percent right. Sean didn't fight. Not with his fists.

"Puerto Ricans are butt," this Black kid told me in fourth grade.

It was three o'clock on the Monday after the Puerto Rican Day Parade. I was outside my school going home when this kid everybody called Hammerhead started teasing me about the Puerto Rican beads I got at the parade. His real name was Gregg. I should've dissed him back about his head because it really popped out in front and back like a hammer. But I didn't think of it. Maybe because I was a little scared. He was bigger than me.

I tried ignoring him but he got louder. Soon, maybe seven kids were walking with him. His friends and other kids, watching.

"Ayo, 'Livin' la Vida Loca,'" Hammerhead shouted at me. "I heard you half Black and half Puerto Rican. What're you? Puerto Rican today? Tomorrow you Black?"

Before I knew it, he was right in front of me. I tried walking around him, but he kept moving to block my way. I didn't know why, but he wanted to fight. Nobody ever jumped in my face like that. My stomach felt funny. My legs started shaking.

Then this voice from the crowd yelled, "Yo, Gregg, why don't you leave Justin alone and go hammer some nails with your forehead."

It was this boy from my building. Sean. We weren't friends. We just passed by and said hi. Probably twice we were on the same volleyball team in gym class. I saw him and his parents around, and then one day his pops was ghost. That was all I knew about Sean until he stepped in between me and Hammerhead.

"Sean," Hammerhead Gregg said. "Mind your business."

"I'm half Puerto Rican, so it is my business. Tease me so I can tell everyone you pooped on yourself last year in class."

"You better be out before I hurt you," Gregg told him.

"You ain't hurting anybody, you piss drinker," Sean yelled for everyone to hear. "Remember in first grade when Derrick dared you to drink piss and you did, nasty?"

"Shut up!" Hammerhead shoved Sean.

Sean pushed him back.

Real quick, kids jumped in between them.

"Get off me," Gregg told his friends.

Sean laughed. "What you gonna do? Becky beat you up last year and she almost put you to sleep with a choke hold. Don't make me go get her right now so she can knock you out again."

Hammerhead tried shaking free and started crying, but his friends held him tighter. "Let me punch him in his face!"

"Stop!" one of Gregg's friends told him. "The principal just came out the school and is looking over here."

"Crybaby," Sean continued with a smile. "You only want to fight because your feelings are hurt. You can't think of a comeback so you want to wrestle me like you're in kindergarten." Sean tapped my chest. "Let's go. Before the principal comes over."

At first I wasn't sure what to do, but I followed Sean. Two blocks away, we stopped at the corner and waited for the crossing guard to let some cars pass. Why'd Sean stick up for me? How come he hadn't been scared back there? Why didn't he stay back there and fight? You're not supposed to walk away from fights. It makes you look soft. Maybe this kid, Sean, was a punk. On the other hand, he made Hammerhead look more butt because he was the one who cried.

"Hammerhead was being mad racist," Sean said

after I finally told him what I was thinking. "I hate that. And I did fight Hammerhead. With my mouth. You better learn how to defend yourself. Listen, my moms says there are four things to remember about fighting. First, people fight when their feelings are hurt. Second, you can fight with your hands or your mouth. Third, people who fight with their hands are too dumb to beat up somebody with their words."

"Yeah," I said. "But you beat up that kid too much. He cried."

"That's the fourth thing," Sean said. "If you beat up a kid with your words, do it so other kids watching get scared of you. If they are, they'll leave you alone. I bet Hammerhead won't say anything to me or you again. Do what my moms said. It works, and that's why I'm not scared of Hammerhead or anybody else."

That was some of the smartest stuff I'd ever heard. Right there, I realized two things.

First, I wanted to be like Sean. I didn't want to fight with my fists. I wanted to beat up people with my words.

Second, I wanted to be Sean's friend.

From that day, I started speaking to Sean more.

Us both being Black and Puerto Rican gave me and him mad similarities. He was completely into hip-hop and a fiend for rap just like me. Soon we had matching black-and-white Composition notebooks to write our rhymes in. We spent mad hours together, listening to music and making verses. We even free-style-rapped with each other. By fifth grade, me and Sean were so close that kids called us twins and brothers from different mothers.

Friends

AFTER HIS DETENTION Sean met me and Vanessa around five o'clock at the handball courts in the stadium. Me, Sean, Kyle, and Vanessa all knew how to play handball, but it was really Sean's sport. Baseball was Kyle's and basketball was Vanessa's. Me? I didn't have one. I guess writing rhymes was more my sport.

It was still light out. Later we were doing a sleepover at Sean's, and Kyle had to stay at home and clean his room if he wanted to be part of it. So right now it was just Sean, me, and Vanessa.

"What happened at detention?" I asked Sean.

Sean sucked his teeth. "Ms. Feeney made me write fifty times, 'I will behave in class.' After that, she gave me a corny speech about how I should know better."

"Manny got detention too?"

"Nope." Sean shook his head, then yelled at this Mexican kid smacking his handball against the wall, "You want singles? I'll play you for your ball."

"Whatever," the kid said.

Our stadium was maybe the size of four football fields. Besides handball courts, it had a track, bleachers, baseball fields, and benches. Trees, little lawns, and paths to walk on. Everywhere, someone played their sport.

The stadium's track had red turf and was maybe half a block from the courts. The track was red like how the planet Mars looked in movies. About ten high school girls in short shorts raced on that track. A chubby Black woman with a tiny Afro in burgundy sweats shouted and blew a whistle at the girls.

I always stayed on the handball courts. A black fence surrounded the eight courts to keep handballs from flying out. Every court had kids, playing or just hanging out. I leaned on the fence next to Vanessa.

Vanessa was full Puerto Rican. Girls acted like she was Alicia Keys. "You got good hair," they'd say, and touch it. They meant straight hair. No naps. Whatever. My hair was nappy and so was Sean's. Kyle's too. Both his parents were Black. Our hair was just as good as Vanessa's.

Vanessa kept her jet-black hair pulled in a bun. A bang hung down the right side of her forehead. Vanessa did remind me a bit of Alicia Keys. She even rocked huge, thin, silver hoop earrings like Alicia wore. I sometimes joked with Vanessa and tried putting my hand through a hoop. She'd punch me in my arm or stomach for that. Quick. Bam.

Right now, Vanessa was staring at Sean. Too hard. Before June she had looked at Sean like they were homeboys. Over the summer, I thought she watched him differently. The way girls did when they thought a guy was cute. I wasn't sure.

"You like Sean," I told her.

She put a face on like she was disgusted. "You stupid."

"Whatever," I said. "Then how come this month you both brought Rollerblades to Field Day in Prospect Park? And skated and held hands?"

To me, that definitely meant Sean liked her. He never held a girl's hand. And I had never seen Vanessa hold a guy's hand before that.

"We did that so we wouldn't fall," she said.

"Dang! Just be honest," I said. "Being friends means we like family. I consider you family. I trust you. You trust me? Then say you like him."

"I don't like him."

"That's it," I said.

"What's it?"

"You and me are fake friends because you lying to me."

"Who cares?" Vanessa turned her back to me. "You don't even know what friendship is."

"You don't either," I said.

I went back to watching Sean. I wished I could ask him if he liked Vanessa. I didn't know how to bring it up or how he'd respond.

Sean was now on the court arguing about the last shot. Was it a killer? Or a choke?

Sean played two more handball games with that Mexican kid before he came over acting all big because he'd beat him. "You got next?" Sean asked, tossing the ball at me.

I caught it and bounced it back at him. "Nah." My mind went back to Ms. Feeney. "I can't believe Ms. Feeney didn't punish Manny too."

Sean smiled and freestyled:

Ayo, Ms. Feeney thinks I'm hotheaded and wants me to cool it.

But she should do her job better. She's stupid and foolish.

I got attacked so I fought back.
She should grab Manny for starting that crap.

Me and Vanessa nodded in beat. Sean let his personality go when he rhymed. Right now he rocked wild, side to side. He waved his arms loose and rhymed:

I got three friends in our little school.
You, Justin. You cool.
Then, let's see . . .
Who completes the three?
There's Kyle and Vanessa.
But V wants to be my wifey.

Sean winked at Vanessa. "Ewww!" Vanessa said, and made a stank face.

Sean laughed at her, then said to me:

Justin, we been peeps since elementary
So why don't you try telling me
Why Ms. Feeney stays grilling me?

Sean stopped rapping and started beatboxing. That was our way of telling each other to join in.

Sean, to tell you the truth,
I have no clue
Why earlier Ms. Feeney got on you

*Because both times today, other kids first tried
playing you.
But she turned around and put that blame on you.
On the flip, though, lunch was sweet
When you dissed that punk and made him leave.*

Sean stopped beatboxing, smiled, and gave me a pound. "True. True."

"I have to go," Vanessa said suddenly. "My mom and dad texted and they want to take me to the movies." Vanessa didn't have brothers or sisters but she had two good parents. Vanessa's father was an electrician. Her mother worked in a hospital. In their free time, they took Vanessa out of Red Hook as much as they could. "You both heading to your block? Or you staying?" Vanessa asked me and Sean.

"We staying," we said.

Vanessa left.

Sean turned around and with both hands gripped the fence and rocked it back and forth real slow. He stared at the Grey House. It was an abandoned building built on a pier next to the stadium. All burned twenty-something floors of it. My mother said that when she moved into Red Hook, the Grey House was a sugar factory and a lot of Red Hook people worked there. When the Grey House burned down, all these different companies wanted to fix it up, do this and that with it. But in the end no companies ever bought it.

But people in Red Hook didn't forget about it for a few reasons. First, the size of the Grey House kept it on people's minds. It was gigantic compared with the pipsqueak buildings around the stadium. It looked almost like a skyscraper. Second, everything in the stadium was new and shiny. Not the Grey House. You could tell its walls used to be white, but now it was stained gray from fire smoke. When we were younger, me and Sean played this game where we took guesses about how many people had died in the Grey House fire. Some kids who went in and came back to our block said the Grey House had ghosts. That just made me and Sean talk even more about the Grey House. We agreed it was the scariest, biggest haunted house ever and talked about different ways we'd sneak in there and how crazy it would be to get on that roof.

"Let's go in there," Sean said right now.

"How?"

"Climb the gate. Cross the junkyard. Sneak in through a broken window."

For a second, I thought he was kidding. But I caught how serious he was, clutching the fence. Like he was fiending to be in the Grey House.

"Nah, I'm not doing it," I told Sean.

"Faggot."

"You the faggot."

"Me?" Sean said. "You the one who's afraid to go in there."

I wasn't sure what to do. I didn't want to climb the Grey House but also didn't want Sean thinking I was a punk.

"Be like that, Justin," Sean said. "Who climbed the gate with you when you wanted to swim in the Red Hook Pool at night?"

I strained hard to see the dogs that were supposed to guard the Grey House, but I didn't spot any. I looked up, and up, and up, to the top. I wondered if we could see Manhattan from the Grey House roof. My mother sometimes took me to Manhattan to museums and parks. Manhattan was mad peaceful.

"If we see dogs, we jet, right?"

"Bet." He smiled.

Once over the gate, we had to cross this junkyard.

"I'll race you inside," I said.

"On your mark. Get set. Go!" Sean said.

We ran fast and I tried not to bust my butt because the ground was slippery with glass and garbage. Burned car parts. Broken bikes. Boxes with trash in them. We got to a window, and as scared as I was, I hopped in first because I still figured a dog might pop out of somewhere. Sean was right behind me. It was dark in the Grey House. The only light came in through the windows. I checked my watch and could barely see the time: 5:45 P.M. I caught something else. My palms were black like I had rubbed charcoal on them. The fire that burned the Grey House must've left ash, and it got on me when I climbed in the window. "This ain't coming off," I said, showing Sean my hands.

"Calm down. It's on me too. We'll wash it off later," Sean said. All of a sudden, his face glowed like a lightbulb. I turned to see what he was looking at. A staircase. It had one step, then two steps missing, then another step, then three steps missing. The staircase was mostly stairless.

"Son, we need to climb that," Sean said.

I had a huge smile and he knew why. I was The Man at climbing. I used to rock-climb up the three-story bread factory behind my building just for fun. I'd squeeze my fingers into cracks in the wall and grip my hands onto poked-out bricks and grab and yank myself up until I stood on the cracker factory roof.

We walked up staircase after staircase. On some floors, only half a staircase went up to the next floor. The other half was missing from the fire. When we found staircases like that, me and Sean walked up as far as we could, then tugged at wires and pipes hanging out walls to see if they felt strong enough to hold our weight. If they didn't snap out the wall, we grabbed them and pulled ourselves to the next floor. We got to the fourteenth floor before we knew it. We looked for a staircase going up to the fifteenth floor but couldn't find one. We wandered into this huge room full of factory machines. Dust on everything. Probably old equipment used back in the day. Light came in through busted windows. Sharp, broken glass stuck out window frames like they could slice somebody's head off. While eyeing the room, I saw on the opposite side a staircase going up to the next floor. That's when I spotted something that scared me. The floor between us and that staircase had huge holes in it. Everywhere. Like heavy equipment had fallen through it. We had to cross this holey floor to get to the staircase.

Sean moved farther into that room.

"Chill." I grabbed his arm. "That floor'll break."

"Relax." He snatched his arm and took another step to see if the floor was solid. He looked at his feet and waited. Nothing. My heart was beating hard. Sean took another step forward and stood still again for two seconds. Nothing happened. Sean took a few steps more into the room. From his new spot, he jumped up and down.

He looked at me and smiled. "See?" he said, waving me to come over. "It's fine."

I slowly stepped halfway to where he was.

"Keep coming!" he yelled.

I moved in closer.

"Now, follow me," he said. He turned and took a step, and the floor broke right underneath him. His legs went straight down until he was showing only from the waist up. I grabbed his forearms type-fast and pulled. But his skin and my hands were slippery from that black charcoal stuff. Sean kept sliding down. He started crying, "Pull me up!"

I had never seen Sean so scared.

I reached for his T-shirt and caught some of it under his armpit. With my other hand, I grabbed a pipe built into the floor. Sean kept slipping deeper into the hole and stuff flashed through my head. Like Sean falling downstairs and breaking his leg. Him laid out with his skull cracked open and bleeding.

Sean's eyes were shut tight and tears ran down his cheeks. He breathed so hard through his mouth that I thought he was having an asthma attack.

I gripped the pipe harder and pulled on his tee and started to cry. Sean came more out the hole. A second later, his hand was next to mine on the pipe. Soon we were laid on the floor, side by side, breathing heavy.

We were there for a minute, calming down. Sean wasn't a scaredy-cat, but he cried. This was the first time I had seen him cry, and he'd never seen me cry before. That's for sure.

"Let's leave," Sean said, standing up slowly. He still looked a little shook.

But when I got up, we noticed something at the same time. Almost hidden underneath pieces of fallen ceiling was a third staircase that went upstairs. We didn't need to cross this holey floor after all. "Maybe the floor's better upstairs," I said.

Sean wiped a tear from his eye with his wrist and put on a serious face. Tough. Maybe to show he wasn't afraid to go to the next floor. "Let's see what's upstairs," he said.

We climbed seven more floors and soon we were at a door. Sean put one hand on the door and shoved it. It squeaked back. Right there, on the twenty-first floor, through that door frame, we saw straight over our housing projects and into Manhattan. The sky was a bit darker now that it was later. I looked at Sean and smiled, but he didn't catch it. He was too busy tapping his foot on the roof to see if it was safe for us to walk on.

"Want to go to the edge?" he asked.

"Nah, man. Nah," I said. "And you not a punk if you don't go neither."

Sean looked at me. He tapped the floor again and thought it over. "If anybody asks, we went to the edge. Cool?"

"I'm not telling anybody we came in here," I said. "My mom'll hit me if she finds out. Let's keep this between me and you."

I knew I was asking Sean for a lot. He was known in our projects and school for not being scared. Asking him to keep our climbing the Grey House secret was like asking LeBron James to lose a game on purpose. Sean probably was dying to jet back and tell everyone we'd done this.

Sean got quiet and looked out at Manhattan for a real long time. I did too. We had a clear view of the city. The tall buildings there were so far away they looked like they could fit in my hand. Watching the Manhattan buildings all lit up was like seeing different parts of a diamond shine.

From the Grey House roof, Red Hook reminded me of Lego toy blocks except the buildings were all brick and tan. Not just the six-story buildings where me and Sean lived. The tall projects in the back of Red Hook looked as small as Lego blocks too. Even though they were fourteen floors high. From where we stood, way above everything, cars on the streets were tiny and moved slow, how ants did. It was nice up there.

I was about to say, "This is hot, right?" but I

noticed Sean's eyes were closed. He inhaled real deep. Maybe he was thinking about something. I closed my eyes and did what I thought he was doing.

"Justin, it's cool," Sean said.

"What's cool?"

"I won't tell anybody we came up here."

For years me and him kept stupid dares we did secret, so I felt I could trust him now. Still, those were little dares. Climbing the Grey House was different. This was one of the craziest things to do in Red Hook. Kids mainly went in the Grey House to brag about it. Me and Sean hadn't just made it in. We'd almost died plus made it to the roof. Sean would be even more The Man if he told kids what happened. For life. I hoped I could trust Sean not to tell. My mom would flip if she found out.

Sean's Secret Trip

AFTER LEAVING THE GREY HOUSE, me and Sean shoved our way through the weeds and junk to a tiny, half-grimy, half-nice beach on the other side of the building. Me and Sean went down to the water but didn't go in. Sean pulled out a shiny metal disc with fancy designs on it from his pocket. After he wiped the dust off, it looked even more rare. Like the cover of a small expensive pocket watch.

"It's from inside," he said. "I snatched it. It's maybe steel, but if you bend it, it might . . ." Sean folded it and it snapped in two. He handed me half.

I ran my thumb over its design and felt the sharp metal edges where it had broken.

"Don't lose that," Sean said. "I'll keep mine."

"Me? Lose mine?" I said. "You'll lose yours before me."

"Want to bet?"

"Bet," I said.

We smiled at each other and headed back to our block.

The door to our building was supposed to stay locked, but as usual the door was open a crack. Drug dealers who didn't live in our building propped a soda-bottle cap in the doorway to keep the door from slamming shut. That way they could get in without a key, handle their business, then leave. I wanted to move the bottle cap so the door could close, but I didn't. What if one of the guys hustling saw me? They might have approached me. So we just went in, stepping over a puddle of piss. It stank. Ammonia strong. Tiny piles of tobacco on the floor here and there. People who smoked weed in our building bought cigars, emptied them, and used the cigar skins to roll blunts. They tossed the cigar tobacco on the floor wherever. They threw their empty nickel bags of weed on the ground too.

Every floor had litter. Graffiti was written on walls with markers or keyed into the paint. On the second floor, a half-drunk Snapple bottle and a Styrofoam coffee cup were on the little bench near the window. Cigarette butts floated in them.

The bottom of my sneaker stuck a little on the floor. I lifted my foot and heard it peel out of whatever sticky liquid it had touched. Maybe spilled Snapple or coffee. Hopefully not piss.

I tried pretending the messiness of my building didn't bother me. Sean did too. In my heart, I wished cops or housing workers kept our stoop door locked and my building safe and clean. Why'd my building have to smell like beer, weed smoke, and piss? At night, people hung in the halls and did their dirt. When I passed them, they looked at me like I was bothering them. My moms and old folks had to walk through this crap. That got me heated too.

Ma told me we were lucky. She said most Red Hook buildings were worse than ours. The worst we ever saw was somebody once got stabbed. But he lived. In a few other buildings, guys were shot and killed.

"It never bugs you how our building is?" I asked Sean.

"Nah," he said. "If it did, I'd go live with my pops in our house in Puerto Rico. It's mad clean there. Like heaven. It's too boring, though."

Right now, I wished I had a cool dad and a house in a nice clean place where me and my moms could live.

My apartment was on the second floor. Sean was on the sixth. When we were in my room, Sean said, "I can only stay an hour or two."

"What?" I said. "I thought I was grabbing my stuff. For our sleepover at your place."

"I forgot to tell you," Sean said. "I can't do our sleepover. My moms said I'm on punishment for not doing my chores."

That was bugged. It wasn't like Sean to cancel a sleepover. I tried not to look upset. Most weekends, me, Sean, and Kyle took turns staying over each other's apartments. The sleepover idea started with me and Sean. After a while, Kyle joined in. Vanessa didn't spend the night at our apartments because a girl staying over boys' houses made her look like a ho. So Vanessa missed out on playing games until three, four in the morning. Us prank-calling kids who went to our school. Watching music videos until we fell asleep.

"Next time," Sean said.

"Word," I answered, but I was confused. I hoped nothing was wrong. It was big for Sean's moms to make him cancel on me and Kyle.

In my room, Sean sat in my beanbag chair and flipped through one of Kyle's rap magazines. Kyle wasn't into rapping as much as me and Sean, but he got rap magazines mailed to his house because his father read *The Source*, *XXL*, and *Vibe*. Kyle knew Sean liked these magazines because they had rappers' rhymes written out. Every month he let Sean borrow the latest issues. They been doing that since fourth grade. That was a way Sean and Kyle were close.

Sean took those magazines and wrote down the rappers' rhymes, twice. A copy for him and one for me. That's how we were close. He could've looked out for just himself but he didn't. Since forever, he hit me off with whatever he got his hands on.

I stood at my CD player. Pressing the skip button and trying to find this battle Black Bald had on BET this past summer.

Black Bald was ill. Me, Sean, Vanessa, and Kyle loved this rapper. We saw him at a free concert in Prospect Park. He battled two other rappers at the same time and he slayed them.

Killah Kid, this rapper I couldn't stand, once popped up on BET and challenged Black Bald right on the show. Killah was a rapper in high school. He had a six-pack stomach and took off his shirt in all his videos. He probably thought he could model. His raps were just okay, but he said he was as good as Jay-Z. Yeah right.

I didn't know who let Killah interrupt Black's

interview on live TV. And I didn't know how Killah got a microphone, but he did.

"Killah," the pretty, Serena Williams–looking host said, surprised. "What you doing here?"

"Why you interviewing this fake?" Killah asked. "Black can't freestyle. He don't even write his own raps." Killah didn't even make eye contact with Black. He turned to the audience instead. "You want to hear me battle this punk?" he asked.

They went crazy. "Battle!" they yelled. "Battle! Battle!"

The female host asked Black, "So you accept Killah's challenge?"

Black took his microphone and waved to the deejay. "Throw on a hot beat. A'ight, Killa. Show us what's good. You first."

Right there on BET, Black ended up ripping Killah. I was fiending to hear that battle again.

"Black killed Killah on what track?" I asked Sean.

"Seven."

I skipped tracks until I got there.

Killah went first:

Hos be flocking me, tricks be jocking me.
I go down the street and chickenheads stay
stopping me.

What about you, Black? You can't bag dimes to save
your life.
With a ugly face like yours only a blind ditz would
be your wife.

The audience went "Oooh" and clapped for Killah.
"Rewind that track," Black said to the deejay. The
beat began again.

Killah, you stay dissing women. Calling them hos,
ditzes, and tricks.
Then you wonder why your last album sold no units.
Why? Because the females you dis didn't go out and
buy your garbage.
Why you need to brag about the women you bag?
And you really shouldn't be coming on BET to
challenge me.
You ain't a real MC. You'll see. You'll get beat.
Plus, I got females in my crew older, taller, and
harder than you.
I should invite one out here to punch two black eyes
on you.

The audience went crazy. Everyone cheered loud.
Through their sounds, I heard the host say to Black,
"You got it. You got it. The audience says you The
Man." That's how that song ended. It faded out to her

voice and claps for Black. I skipped to Track 9. Black rapped:

I didn't have a pops. Just a moms to admire.
She loved me nonstop even when I made her stressed and tired.

I skipped to Track 12. Black went:

Gina from my way liked guys who gave her strife.
If Gina was my girl, I would've shown her the good life.

For some reason I thought about Sean. Maybe because I never heard him dis girls. Or probably from how he treated Vanessa. Never put her down. I asked him, "Why you think Black never disses women the way other rappers do?"

Without taking his eyes off Kyle's magazine, Sean said, "Probably because he knows a cool female he trusts."

"You trust girls?" I asked.

"I trust Vanessa."

"Really?"

"No doubt." Sean strained hard at something on a page. "Vanessa's good people."

I knew Sean had something with Vanessa but he wouldn't admit it. But I didn't know he felt close enough to her to trust her with stuff. I thought he trusted only me. What Sean had just said about Vanessa made me think. What little side conversations did they have that I didn't know about? Did things I told Sean get back to Vanessa? I asked Sean, "What kind of stuff you trust Vanessa with?"

Sean flipped Kyle's magazine shut. I could tell he realized he'd slipped and now was wondering how much to tell me. Sean scratched the back of his head and said, "Nothing big. Remember last year? When my moms was sick for all them days?"

"Yeah."

"On the first day she felt bad," Sean said, "she sent me to the store to buy medicine and I bumped into Vanessa. I told her my moms didn't feel good. She went with me to the supermarket and then came back to my apartment. She sat that day with my moms, the next day, and every day after that. Vanessa checked on my mother until she got better. From then on, my moms loved Vanessa. And I learned Vanessa is all right. Now and then, I trust her with little things. With nothing major, though."

The way he said "nothing major" made me wonder if Sean had any big secrets I didn't know about. I thought he told me everything, but what he'd just said made me feel like he was keeping stuff from me.

"You should ask her out," I said.

Sean's face turned so serious it wasn't funny. "Black probably respects females because he knows someone cool like Vanessa," he said, then went back to reading the magazine.

I watched Sean for a second. His face was still a little red and he obviously didn't want to talk no more so I took the Black Bald disc out and put the radio on.

Sean said he couldn't be around for our sleepover, and later that night he wasn't. It was just me and Kyle in my room at two in the morning.

"Do you urinate frequently?" the man on TV asked. The wildest commercials came on TV late at night. "If you're sixty-five or older and you can't control your bladder, this commercial is for you."

I sat on my bed with my back against my wall. "What you think about this commercial?" I asked Kyle.

He was in my wheelie chair at my desk, playing on my computer. Kyle stopped, spun toward the TV, took one finger, and pushed his glasses up his nose. He did that whenever he was figuring something out. Kyle nodded twice. "It's whatever, whatever." He got back on the computer.

I switched channels.

Trying to stay up with Kyle without Sean was kind of wack. Kyle was the quietest of us. Laid-back. He didn't rush into things and didn't get excited fast. He thought maybe three times before speaking or acting once. I respected how he thought deep about things because I could be that way too. But Kyle was that way 24/7. His mood was "Do you, I do me. Mind your business, I mind mine." At other times, I liked being more like Sean. Sean could just be wild. Since Kyle couldn't be that way, trying to bug out with him right now was tough.

"Fifty-two shots and all you cats drop. Pop. Pop. Pop. Don't even step on my block."

Finally! I found something good on television. Black's new video. "Yeah, Black!" I said.

Kyle was feeling the video because he nodded to Black's beat. He made his voice low like how Black sounded and rapped Black's rhyme:

You wanna come to where I rest and disrespect?
Punk, you'll get checked, wrecked. I'll break your neck.

I made my voice as deep as Kyle's and jumped in to rap Black's next part with him. Kyle turned around to face me, and it was almost like we were battling, barking Black's words at each other:

You on the wrong side of the tracks.
Trace back your footsteps to where you live at
Before you get smacked and jacked.

On that last word, me and Kyle started laughing. I didn't know why. We just did.

"Oh man," Kyle breathed out hard. "That was fun." But then he went back to playing his game.

But I was still pumped from rapping and wanted to keep going. You corny, Kyle, I thought. Back on the computer. If he'd been Sean, he wouldn't have done that. Me and Sean probably would've started free-styling. Made up our own rhymes. Had a rap battle.

I wondered if Sean was up right now. I had energy and didn't know what to do with it. I changed channels until I found another video I liked.

"Kyle, you saw this one?" I was about to raise the volume when I looked at my digital clock. It was 2:15 in the morning. My mom would flip if I turned it up.

I left the volume alone.

Out my window I heard the stoop door slam, but nobody was there when I checked. Sometimes, at four, five in the morning, you didn't need to watch TV to stay up. Just watch my stoop. People argued and fought down there. Drunks, crackheads, drug dealers.

Right now, I couldn't tell if the stoop door slamming meant drama.

Kyle was laid out on my bed. Asleep. Even though the television was on. His eyes half open and rolled up in his head. He maybe could sleep through a fire. I turned off the television and there was another slam. I went back to the window. What I saw bugged me out.

"Sean, baby." Sean and his mom stepped off the stoop. "Wake up."

Sean was half asleep and standing wobbly like he was about to fall over. His mother put one hand under his arm to hold him up. She had a small suitcase in her other hand. Tiny enough for a weekend trip. I backed a bit out of the window so they wouldn't see me.

What's up with that? Sean had told me he would be around this weekend on punishment. Why were they leaving? Did they have a family emergency?

"Come on, Sean," Jackie said. She took him by the hand and led him off the court. They disappeared behind a building.

I wanted to wake up Kyle and tell him what I had just seen, but all these thoughts were going through my head. Did Sean know he was bouncing this weekend? Yes or no? He never went somewhere without telling me first. Where were they going at so early in the morning? With a suitcase?

I let Kyle sleep and decided not to tell him what I had just seen. Maybe because I didn't want to hear Kyle say something like, "We should mind our own business." I wasn't in the mood to hear that, because I was worried about Sean. He didn't look like he knew where his mom was taking him. Was she taking him somewhere to leave him?

The Morning After

THE NEXT MORNING, Kyle didn't stay for breakfast. He pitched for a Little League team and they had a game that day. His parents were the coaches and picked him up early from my place.

After brushing my teeth, I sat at our breakfast table while Ma cooked. I was there with no video game. No nothing. Just me hunched, confused about why Sean had snuck out last night and hadn't said where he was going.

"What's bugging you?" Ma asked.

"Nothing," I said, but she wasn't stupid.

The pancakes on the stove sizzled. Usually I couldn't wait to eat them. But right now Ma's food didn't faze me.

"Justin, if I looked like this"—Ma puffed her cheeks and folded her arms—"would you say nothing is wrong with me?"

I smiled. I didn't think I looked like that.

"At least I'm not wearing slippers five sizes too big for me," I joked.

"If you want me making pancakes and eggs for you like I do every Saturday morning, I'm cooking them in my clown slippers." Ma stuck her tongue out at me.

I laughed.

Ma's black hair was curled in rollers. Pink ones. Matching her pink, fluffy bathrobe. Ma liked her pajamas loose-fitting. Her collar was turned up and the sash around her waist was tied in front.

She scooped two pancakes from the pan, slid them onto a plate of steaming scrambled eggs, and set that in front of me.

"So what's bothering you?" There. Ma was picking at me again.

"I just feel like being quiet."

But Ma hated it when I didn't speak for a long time and sat angry.

"Guys out here get taught from little to act hard," she would say. "They're supposed to pretend nothing is wrong with them. They think they can't ever be sensitive because that's considered soft or gay. So these boys and men out here bottle in their real feelings. Wearing armor and fronting. But being hard only leads to trouble. Feelings explode out and lots of guys are in jail, hooked on drugs, and dead for being hard."

Ma used to have three brothers. It was her, Robby, Craig, and Josh. My uncles were hard. Now all of them are dead or locked up. Robby sold drugs and got shot in the head when he was in high school. Craig caught HIV sharing needles and died at twenty-two. Uncle Josh is alive and in jail for life because he was a gang leader out here and had somebody killed. He was my only uncle and once Ma took me upstate to see him, but on the bus ride home she told me, "I'm not taking you back to see him. I'm not getting you used to being inside a jail. Josh chose that life for him. I didn't choose jail for you." And just like that, we never visited Uncle Josh again.

After Ma's mother and father died, it was just her. Alone. Out here in Red Hook. Maybe I have uncles on my father's side, but I've never met anyone from my father's side because they live down south, and Ma said, "If they're not coming up here, we're not going down there." It sucks not having a father or uncle, because I see boys out here playing football and doing things with their dads and uncles. I have to do that stuff with my mother. Which is cool. But kind of gay too.

Ma grabbed a plate out the cupboard. "You feel like being quiet. Fine. So maybe I feel like not telling you what I saw last night."

I asked, "What you see?"

"I'll tell you one thing"—she flipped a pancake over and pointed the spatula at me—"if you tell me one thing?"

"Okay."

She said, "Sean."

"And his mother," I said.

"Yep," Ma said. "I woke up around two-something and couldn't go back to sleep. At four in the morning, I heard the stoop door slam and I looked outside. That's when I saw Jackie and Sean. Where were they going?"

"I don't know." I felt stupid saying that to Ma.

"Sean didn't tell you?" She looked at my face and checked for something. Ma probably thought, What type of best friends are you and Sean? Or maybe she felt I was lying.

"No," I said. "He didn't say." I could tell when Ma thought I was lying to her. She would wrinkle her nose a certain way and shake her head. She didn't do it this time.

"Mmm." Ma turned back to the stove and flipped over another pancake. "I hope everything's okay."

"Maybe Sean will say where he went when he gets

back," I told her. "If he doesn't, that's cool." When things bothered me, Ma didn't want me keeping that stuff to myself. She didn't like if I avoided telling my guy friends how they bugged me. Ma hated that because she said I was acting hard. She felt that only made problems worse.

"So what if Sean doesn't tell you where he went?" Ma asked.

I grabbed my fork and cut a piece of pancake. I hoped that by the time I swallowed and looked up, Ma would be focused back on the stove and not on me. I gulped down my food and checked. She was still staring at me. Dead in my eyes. I shrugged. "I'll be fine if he doesn't tell me."

"Justin," Ma said, all serious. "Look at me. If Sean doesn't tell you where he went and you have a problem with that, you better ask him." She kept her eyes on me for a second and then turned back to cooking.

Sean Acts Weird

A FEW TIMES ON SATURDAY AND SUNDAY I CALLED SEAN. Nobody picked up his house phone or cell. On Monday, we didn't come to school together because he never answered his phones. I didn't see him until fourth period in gym.

First, our gym teacher, Mr. K, made us put our stuff in lockers. Then we sat on the floor while he took attendance. After that, he let us have "free play." While we were on the floor, I looked over at Sean. He nodded to me.

"What up?" Sean yelled after Mr. K finished taking attendance.

You needed to shout in gym because the sound of kids was everywhere.

"What up," I said. "What time you came to school?"

"Second period."

That's an hour after school started. Sean had perfect attendance. He never came to school late. So what was up with him coming to school second period?

I opened my mouth to ask him where he had bounced to this weekend, but a bunch of kids we played dodgeball with ran up. Plus two eighth graders we had never played with before. Mark and Junito. Mark was Sean's older cousin, but they weren't close. Jackie didn't like how her sister had no rules in her apartment. Mark was off-the-hook wild.

"What's good?" Mark asked Sean.

"What up, Sean," Junito said.

Sean nodded and gave them pounds. "I'll come see you at the bleachers after I'm done with dodgeball."

What? Sean was going to the bleachers to hang with them? Why?

Sean had grabbed the dodgeball before we sat for attendance. As Mark and Junito walked off, this kid Big Eddie came over and snatched the ball from Sean's hands. We sometimes called Eddie that because he was in the sixth grade but he was as big as an eighth grader. He even had a light mustache and caveman hairy arms. Maybe he'd been left back a few times. Maybe not. I saw his pops once. His father looked like Big Foot.

Big Eddie bounced the ball he had just snatched. "I'm captain."

I get heated when people snatch things from me. That's like punking someone. But Sean didn't mind stuff like that.

"Bet," Sean said. "But I choose first."

Sean picked me for his team. Big Eddie chose this quiet dark-skinned West Indian boy in our class. Soon Sean and Eddie were shouting and pointing at kids so fast that we had two teams quicker than you could count to five.

The teams ran to opposite sides.

When the ball came to our side, Sean got it and threw it mad hard at Miguel. It was like a cannon shot it. Everybody dove out the way.

Some kid let it bounce, and then he picked it up and threw it back.

The ball hit the floor next to me. I grabbed it and flung it. I caught some kid who wasn't looking. In the face! He was dazed like he saw birds chirping.

"You out!" I yelled.

The kid went and stood on the sidelines.

"Good one," Sean said.

Ask Sean now, I thought. Nah. The timing was off. I decided to wait until dodgeball ended.

When the game was over, Sean walked toward the bleachers and I followed him.

"Where you went this weekend?" I asked.

"I told you," Sean said. "My mom had me on lock-down. Doing chores."

"What about your phones?" I asked. "I called your house and cell. Nobody answered."

Sean shrugged and squinted hard at something far off. "I lost my cell battery. I don't know what happened with my house phone."

"And your mother?" I asked. "She didn't hear your house phone ring?"

"Oh!" Sean said. "I almost forgot! My mom was on it a lot with my pops. Maybe she didn't click over when you called because she was on long-distance with him?"

Mark ran up on us. "Ayo, Sean. Come tell Junito and Eric that deadbeat dad joke you told me earlier."

After Sean left with Mark, I felt like Sean had just treated me like we weren't friends. Why couldn't Sean look me in the eye? I wondered. Ma always said liars avoid eye contact.

I went to find Vanessa and Kyle. Vanessa was playing basketball. I decided not to stop her game.

Especially after hearing Sean say how him and her had some special friendship. I didn't know how she'd respond. I checked for Kyle. He was on one knee and about to race two kids from our class. Bony Charles with the braces and dark-skinned Vicky, who always kept her hair in neat braids with rainbow-colored beads at the ends.

"Don't keep your thoughts and feelings bottled in," I could hear my mother saying. Before, I thought Kyle would tell me to mind my business. Right now I wanted him to do me a favor. "On your mark, get set . . . ," Kyle began.

I put my hands up and stopped the race. "Kyle! I need to tell you something!"

"What?" Kyle asked. His forehead was dripping sweat.

"Come on. We racing or what?" Bony Charles said.

"Relax," Kyle said to him. "I just raced you twice and beat you. Wait."

Me and Kyle moved over to the volleyball net. Kids were playing volleyball all wrong.

"What's good?" Kyle asked me.

"I need to tell you something. Don't tell Vanessa. Sean just lied to me, I think."

"Really? How you know?"

I wasn't ready to tell him I knew Sean had lied because I saw him leave early Saturday morning. "You remember how I once told you my mom said liars can't stare you in the face when they lie?" I said. "That they always look away?"

"Yeah."

"Sean did that. Go over to him and his new best eighth-grade friends and ask him what he did this weekend. Watch how he acts. I bet you a dollar he won't make eye contact with you."

Kyle looked over at Sean. "No bet. I'm not going over there to see if Sean is lying. If he is, he has his reason. That's his business, not mine."

"Do it for me then. Go see how Sean acts with you. For me."

Kyle gave me a stank look and twisted his lips to the side. "Fine. Be right back." He ran over to Sean and Mark's eighth-grade crew. It took Kyle only a minute to get back. "You right. Sean was weird. He didn't look me in the eye."

I stood there. Confused. "Sean's lying."

"Okay, he's lying," Kyle said. "So what?"

I had nothing to say.

"Thought so," Kyle said. "I'm out. I'll be racing."

I went over to the pull-up bar on the opposite side of the gym from Sean. Sean's acting different, was all I could think. Why was he lying? Where was he going? Why at four in the morning?

Enough Is Enough

SEAN WAS TWO LUNCH TABLES DOWN FROM US. He was laughing with his cousin Mark, Junito, and some more eighth graders who were about nothing.

I checked Kyle's face. Kyle was looking at Sean too. Analyzing him.

Vanessa, on the other hand, was eating her spaghetti and meatballs and humming a song. She was into her food. Forget her.

Now I was ready to pull Kyle to the side and tell him about Sean's secret Saturday trip. But I couldn't do that. That would make me a snitch.

An idea popped into my head. If Sean backed out of another sleepover, I'd get Kyle to stay over my place. We'd bust Sean, and Kyle would get curious. That would lead to us approaching Sean. Two people saying something is different than one person snitching. I'd feel better confronting Sean with Kyle there. I'd be less nervous speaking up, knowing Kyle was there to back me up.

But maybe none of that would happen, I thought. Maybe Sean wouldn't even sneak out again.

Over the next few weeks, me, Sean, Vanessa, and Kyle did the usuals. Hung out in our lunchroom. Gym. Met after school, did homework, and played games. But Sean wasn't always the usual Sean. Sometimes, he was mad different and took his meanness to a whole other level. When he acted that way, it was hard for me to feel normal with him.

One day at the beginning of science class, he pulled this kid George's chair from underneath him.

Our teacher didn't see Sean do it.

"I'll get you back." George fake-laughed.

But him, me, and Sean knew he was too scared of Sean to do anything.

The next day, Sean pulled Richard's chair as he sat in math.

"Stop," Richard said.

Sean winked and smiled at me like I was supposed to think what he just did was funny, but I didn't smile back. I was too busy wondering what was wrong with him. First, yesterday with George and now Richard? What if one of them fell and got hurt? Plus, what if a teacher busted Sean? I was more worried about Sean getting in trouble than he cared himself.

Every day, in the halls, when he walked behind boys and they didn't see him, Sean tossed the gum from his mouth into their hair or hoodies. He never used to bother kids for no reason. Now it was like every time he was around other kids, he had to be mean.

I was annoyed with Sean. Kyle was too. Before, Kyle used to laugh at all of Sean's jokes. Not anymore.

That week me and Kyle saw him be mean and we'd just stare at each other and suck our teeth like we were saying, "He's bugging."

Once the hall was mad crowded as me and Sean headed to lunch. He snuck behind this boy Kenneth and kicked him in the butt.

"Yo!" Kenneth swung around. "Who kicked me?"

Sean pointed at someone else. "He did."

I could tell from Kenneth's face that he guessed Sean did it, but he pretended he didn't have a clue because he knew Sean would embarrass him if Kenneth tried to act brave.

"That was mad funny," Sean said to me, putting his fist out for a pound. "You saw Kenneth's face?"

"Nah." I shook my head. "That wasn't funny," and I left Sean hanging.

"You soft," Sean said.

Yeah, he definitely wasn't the old Sean.

Me, Sean, and Kyle kept doing our sleepovers.

Weeks later, almost at the end of October, me and Kyle slept over Sean's. It was late and we were bored, doing nothing. Right then, I decided to entertain myself. In elementary school he collected Yu-Gi-Oh! cards like crazy. Sean didn't see me get out the shoe box he kept them in because he was busy playing with his new iPhone.

Yo! More was in his shoe box than just Yu-Gi-Oh! cards. Sean had a bunch of dollar bills in there. I scooped them and counted them.

"Sean, where you get almost fifty dollars from?" I asked him.

Before Sean could answer, Kyle jumped up and took the money from me. "Son!" he told Sean. "You got money like that? Give me five bucks."

Real fast, Sean hopped out of his desk chair and snatched his money from Kyle. "My pops sent me this," then paused, "from Puerto Rico." He switched the conversation quick. "Let's go watch videos in my living room."

He had made his lying move. Either he didn't get

that money from his dad or something else about what he said was a lie.

I looked at Kyle funny like "What's up with him and this money?" but we already knew he got money from his dad, so Sean's fifty dollars could be no big deal. Besides, right now, I got more hyped about Sean's giant flat-screen TV. I always liked watching it because it was as big as some televisions I saw in mansions on MTV *Cribs*. We dragged Sean's beanbags from his room and plopped them on his living-room floor.

Sean flicked his remote until he found a 50 Cent video on music-on-demand. I felt like a rich kid watching this TV. Me, him, and Kyle started nodding to 50 when Sean's mom came out her bedroom.

"Hey, guys," she said all sweet to me and Kyle, but then she switched to a stank tone. "Whattup, bighead?" she said to Sean.

Her voice and dis on Sean shocked me. I wondered if they were pissed at each other. Their faces didn't change at all. Sean kept his eyes on the video, but then said back, "You a bighead," with no feeling.

Jackie wasn't fazed. She kept walking and disappeared into the kitchen.

Kyle didn't pay them any mind. He was as focused as Sean on the video.

Sean and his mom were bugged. My mom never

called me names. Plus, Ma wouldn't let me. If I dissed her, she'd smack me.

I thought back to when Sean walked into Ms. Feeney's Advisory and said that gang guy was a "bighead." I wondered where he got that from. Now I knew. Sean's mom was calling him bighead.

The next weekend was Halloween weekend. Sean and Kyle slept over my place, but Sean came over late.

"Sorry," Sean said to us, taking his jacket off. "My dad called from Puerto Rico to wish me a happy Halloween. My mom made me stay and talk to him."

I felt a little jealous. Since my pops bounced, he never called me. Not on my birthday, not on holidays. I barely remembered how his voice sounded. I wondered if he'd even recognize my voice on the phone.

"It's cool," I said.

"Don't worry about it," Kyle said. "You here now."

My mother always was a nervous wreck on Halloween. Since I was little, she'd said, "This holiday is some people's excuse to act dumb." She was scared I'd get hurt because kids in Red Hook went egging. Sometimes, kids threw eggs at you from their windows or roofs. Then they hid. Some troublemakers took egging to another level and hard-boiled the eggs so their eggs felt like rocks when they hit someone.

Other kids traveled in groups and egged you right in the open, then dared you to do something. I saw fistfights break out because the wrong kid got egged and came back with a crew of friends, uncles, or cousins. On some Halloweens, to avoid drama, Ma took me out of the projects to safe neighborhoods. Carroll Gardens. Park Slope. Brooklyn Heights. There, cops were walking around everywhere on Halloween. People felt safe enough to sit right on their stoops with their house doors open. They smiled and gave candy to trick-or-treaters who passed by. No egging in those neighborhoods.

This year, my mom wasn't in the mood to take me, Kyle, and Sean out of Red Hook because her leg was acting up. When it was about to rain, she got pains. Kyle and Sean didn't want to go trick-or-treating anyway. They said we were sixth graders now and too big to ask for candy like little fifth graders.

Half of me agreed. Another part of me was into wearing costumes and getting free candy. I didn't tell Kyle or Sean my thoughts, though. They'd already said, "Trick-or-treating is for kids smaller than us." If I said how I felt, they might tease me and call me a little kid.

After school, we bought our own bags of candy, and that night we stayed up watching scary movies on cable and dogging all our treats. When the movies ended, we made up our own corny ghost stories. We did that over and over until we fell asleep.

Things felt back to normal. Sean wasn't cracking on kids so much anymore.

The weekend after that, me and Sean were supposed to sleep over at Kyle's. Friday morning came. While me and Sean were on the bus, he said, "I can't do the sleepover." He squinted out the bus window at something. He shrugged and, without looking at me, said, "My mom is having her friends over. She wants me around."

Was he lying to me again? I couldn't take him lying to me again.

We got off the bus and Sean shouted at one of his older friends. "Rob. Wait up."

"Sean," I said. "Before we go over there, hold on."

"What up, Justin?"

The words on my tongue. I wanted to say, "I saw you and your mother sneak out weeks ago. Is she really having friends over this weekend? Or you lying again?" But I rethought asking Sean that. He could be telling the truth now because he had missed only one sleepover before.

"Yeah?" Sean asked.

"Nothing," I said.

"Cool. Let's go see Rob."

Cool? Was me and Sean really "cool"? He was dissing me and Kyle again. I was tight. Me and Kyle should stay up late and spy on Sean, I thought. Find out if he's really sneaking out. But I had to be smart with that. I couldn't just approach Kyle and say, "Let's spy on Sean." I was so in my head that I missed Sean leave. He was already three cars away, talking to Mark. We were supposed to go over there together. He didn't even stop to check if I was coming.

He said something to Mark and they started laughing. I sucked my teeth because seeing them act close got me even tighter.

At lunch, Sean and Vanessa went to the soda machine. It was the first time I had been alone with Kyle all day. I put my cheeseburger down and wiped my mouth with a napkin. "Sean can't do the sleepover," I said.

"Really? How come?"

"Something about his mom having her friends over. What about you? You still down?"

"No doubt."

My next words came out so fast I didn't even remember thinking them. "How about we sleep over my place tonight?"

"Sure," Kyle said. "But why?"

"No reason." I picked up my chocolate milk, sipped,

and looked over to the soda machine. Sean and Vanessa were coming back. I grabbed my cheeseburger but kept my eyes on them.

My mind went back to the real reason I wanted Kyle sleeping over my place. Now me and Kyle could stay up late and spy on Sean. Once we both saw him, we could blow up Sean's spot. I was still too scared to approach Sean alone, but I couldn't wait for tonight. I bit into my burger.

And Again . . .

AT FOUR IN THE MORNING, I stuck my head out my window. It was dark and the block was dead. I listened carefully. Something moved near my stoop so I stared there.

"Who you spying on?" Kyle asked. He was at my TV playing Hunt or Be Hunted. In it, you kill aliens before they reach and destroy your city. When you shoot them, they splat into green slime.

"No one," I said, but I kept looking near my stoop. A stray cat busted out a cardboard box and jetted across my block. That made my heart jump.

I got out of the window and watched Kyle blast two more aliens.

"I guess you don't want to play this," he said.

I snatched my remote and zapped my radio on.

"Oooh. Wanna keep you happy, baby. Keep you happy, baby." That song from that blazing female singer Lady Dee, who belly-danced, was on.

"Holla!" I stood up and joked like I was dancing with Lady Dee. "Dee's my girl!"

"You stupid." Kyle laughed. "How she your girl when she mine?" He started humming and head-nodding to her song.

The stoop door outside slammed.

I flung the remote on my bed and flew to the window. Nothing.

"Damn, son." Kyle paused his game and came over. "What you fiending to see?"

"Shh," I hushed him.

I knew Sean was about to come off our stoop with his mother. I could feel it.

The stoop door slammed again. A'ight! This was it.

"I'll pay you back tomorrow," this crackhead said, and walked all dramatically off my stoop, her flip-flops slapping the ground. Ugh, I thought. Where's Sean? A teenager who sold drugs in my building be-bopped off the stoop behind the crackhead. He had a scarf wrapped on his head with his gang colors. The same color scarf hung out his jeans' back pocket. "You better," he said. He scanned around to see if anybody saw him hustling. Me and Kyle quickly got out of the window. I turned and looked at the digital clock on my dresser. Four twenty-five in the morning.

Man, I don't even know why I stayed up. Sean wasn't taking a secret Saturday trip again. I felt stupid.

I went and unpaused Kyle's game and blasted an alien. I used the gun feature and switched my shotgun for an Uzi. This time, I squeezed and splattered six aliens at the same time. That felt good.

"Justin," Kyle said. I turned, but all I could see was his back because his head was out my window. "You won't believe who's out here."

I rushed over. Sean and his mother were there. She had the suitcase. Sean had his half-asleep look on again.

Jackie grabbed Sean's hand and we watched her lead him until they disappeared.

"Whoa," Kyle said. "Do you know where Sean's going? He tell you?"

"No."

"Where he goes is his business." Kyle shook his head. "Still, this is crazy. Sean's a straight liar."

I felt torn in two. One part of me was like, "Yes!" because my plan was working out. I got Kyle to see Sean sneak out. Another piece of me felt low. The last person I wanted to double-team and force to tell me the truth was Sean. Sean was my dog. You just don't gang up on your best friend. But was he my best friend? If Sean was my boy, he would've put me on to where he was heading right now. This was mad stressful. Worrying about Sean and what to do next made my palms sweaty.

What's Up With Sean?

WE DIDN'T HEAR FROM SEAN OVER THE WEEKEND. On Monday, we didn't see him on our way to school, but he was there in gym.

We sat on the floor waiting for Mr. K to finish taking attendance. Sean sat Indian-style seven kids behind me. The dodgeball was in his lap. When he saw me, he gave me a slo-mo nod. He seemed out of it. Maybe from his last trip? Kyle was two rows of kids over from me.

"Dodgeball?" I mouthed to Sean.

Sean gave me a thumbs-up.

"Okay!" Mr. K yelled. "Free play!"

Me and Kyle jetted in Sean's direction.

"Sean, why you tight?" I asked.

71

"I'm mad tired. My mom had her friends over," he told me as he gave Kyle then me a five. "Justin, you knew that."

"Be honest with your boys. Don't bottle in your feelings." I remembered that advice from Ma. I wanted to say, "Your mother didn't have friends over."

But just as I built up my confidence to say it, that sixth grader Big Eddie with the light mustache and caveman hairy arms ran over to us and grabbed at the ball Sean had. Sean yanked it back. Hard.

"Nah, son!" Sean said. Pissed. "My ball first."

Sean's voice was so angry you would've thought Eddie had done something really wrong, but he had only tried grabbing the dodgeball. He had done that to Sean before and Sean hadn't said anything. This time, Sean eyed him like if Eddie touched the ball again, he would knock Eddie's front teeth down his throat. Big Eddie's a foot taller than Sean but he backed off. Like most boys we know, he's scared of Sean.

"Let's go!" Sean snapped at him, and stormed off toward the dodgeball area.

Eddie paused a second. He looked at us, not knowing what to do next because Sean had just punked him, but in the end he followed Sean across the gym.

"What's up Sean's butt?" Kyle asked. "You think his trip pissed him off?"

"You asking me?"

Sean's cousin Mark and some of Sean's new eighth-grade friends played dodgeball with us. Junito, Tony, and David.

When dodgeball was over, Sean didn't speak to me or Kyle. He walked by us and went to the bleachers with his eighth-grade crew.

"Sean's tight, huh?" Kyle said.

"Seriously." We both eyed Sean. "What you think is bothering him?"

"I think he needs to see a counselor." Kyle pushed his glasses up his nose and crossed his arms. "I'm a little worried about him. What you think?"

It shocked me to hear him say that. I couldn't remember the last time I heard a boy worry about another boy without being called homo. "You playing or you serious?" I asked Kyle. "You really worried about him?"

"Forget it," he said, turning a bit away from me. "Let's go play basketball. One-on-one. If I win, I get your lunch. You win, you take mine."

"Chill," I said. "Let's finish this about Sean."

"Nah," Kyle said. "We focused on him but he's over there not even thinking about us."

"I'm worried about him too," I said fast, hoping Kyle would open up if he knew I felt the same way.

"Good for you," Kyle said, walking away.

I wanted to talk more about Sean but it was pointless. Kyle's mouth was now super-glued shut and he'd probably stay that way.

"Alright then," I yelled as I caught up to him. "Me versus you for lunch and grab me a chocolate milk since you'll be losing."

"Whatever," he said.

Me and Kyle went to find Mr. K to get an extra basketball. As we did, I quickly eyed Sean at the bleachers. I still couldn't believe he had walked right by us.

The days right before Thanksgiving break, our parents did the usuals to get ready for the holiday. Except for Sean's mom. The supermarkets where Red Hook people shopped stayed packed with families grabbing turkeys, cranberry sauce, stuffing, and other things. On Monday, me and Ma saw Vanessa and her mom in Fairway. The next day Kyle's parents came pushing their shopping cart toward me and my mother while we were in C-Town's soda and chips aisle. Not once that week did I see Sean and his mom shop. That was weird. Every year around this time I bumped into him and Jackie in at least one store in our neighborhood. If not Fairway, then C-Town. If not C-Town, then Pathmark.

On Wednesday, in English class, our teacher let

us stretch for a minute before we did independent reading. While Sean was over at the bookshelf, I asked if his mom was being late with her shopping.

Without looking at me, he said, "We not shopping because we going to Philly." He made his lying move again. This time, his face was almost angry as he tried hard not to make eye contact with me. I wanted to ask him if everything was okay, but there wasn't time. "Everyone, back to your seats," our teacher yelled.

At my table, I thought about Sean going to Pennsylvania. Even though he had made his lying move before, I guessed maybe he was telling the truth about Philly, because Jackie had a friend there, and Sean's room had pictures and key chains from the times he had gone. I started to wonder if that was where he had bounced to those times he ditched our sleepovers.

Our teachers were happy about the holiday just like people in our projects. Classrooms, doors, and our school's hallway walls were hooked up with pictures of turkeys, Indians and Pilgrims, and colorful signs that said, "Happy Thanksgiving." A few times me and Sean passed those things and I caught him roll his eyes at them. He had never done that before.

That same week I saw Sean switch up in other ways. When he was with just me and Kyle, he spoke less. Always stuck in his head. I tried rhyming a few times with Sean to open him up. Each time I did, he said, "Nah. I don't feel like rhyming."

The Monday before Thanksgiving break about ten seventh and eighth graders huddled in a circle outside the school library. From down the hall I could tell they were freestyling. Somebody was beatboxing. Words were flowing. I got to the crowd and squeezed my way almost to the center to see who was rapping. It was Sean. Standing opposite him were his cousin Mark and Mark's homeboy Kevin waiting their turn to freestyle back. Sean wasn't facing me so he didn't see me, and I didn't want him to.

In school, some boys who weren't as popular as Sean acted as if one hi from him made them cooler. Before his trips Sean nodded back at them and even gave them pounds. But the Tuesday before the break me and him went from math class to science and this kid Jeremy passed, gave Sean his hand, and said, "What's good?"

Sean reached his hand toward Jeremy's, but just as he got close, Sean shaped his hand like a gun and shot Jeremy's hand. "Bongh! Bongh!"

Jeremy took his hand back, looking punked.

"Get out of here, you bighead," Sean said.

Jeremy left with a hurt face on.

It was a short week but every day Sean was dissing somebody, even handicapped kids—kids in wheel-chairs, on crutches, and some who were as big as grown-ups but acted the way babies did. On Wednes-day, me and Sean were on the way to lunch and a bunch of those kids were waiting for the elevator with their teacher.

"Ayo, cripples, do the crip walk," Sean said to them.

He spoke loud enough for the kids' teacher to hear. He was lucky she was busy reading her *Daily News*. If she had heard him, he would've gotten in trouble. What was wrong with him? He never picked on handicapped kids. Now it was like Sean made fun of any kid with something wrong with them.

Another big change I caught was how lately Sean's disses were always a lot meaner.

At our lunchroom table, Sean asked one kid, "Peter, how's your father? Oops, I forgot. You don't have one."

That same day on the third floor, we passed a water fountain and Sean told this kid sipping water, "William, don't get too close to that faucet. Somebody might bump into you. Knock your teeth out. Then you'll look like your dad."

Seventh period, we went down a packed stairwell and Sean yelled at this kid Brian. "Brian! Is that a new shirt?!" Sean snapped. "Where you getting new clothes from? Aren't you on welfare because your dad bounced?"

A few times I wanted to ask Sean what was wrong with him. I felt a little bad when he made welfare jokes because I was on welfare. Plus, why was he bullying? But he was becoming so quiet with me that I thought telling him what was on my mind would make him switch off completely and stay cold with me.

Sean treated Vanessa the opposite of how he was with me. He was thirsty to talk to her.

When school let out for Thanksgiving, kids were hanging out everywhere on the block, happy to have two days and a weekend off. They shouted and ran this and that way. In the streets, cars and yellow school buses honked at kids who jaywalked. I spotted two security guards clearing students off the sidewalk. "Go home! Everybody away from the school," they shouted.

Me, Sean, Kyle, and Vanessa left the building. I stopped for a second near some parked cars because I wanted to talk about our science homework. Science was no joke. It was getting harder and harder.

"What you get on the last science test?" I asked Sean, trying to start a conversation.

"Fifty-five."

"What?" I said, shocked.

"It's nothing." Sean shrugged, then leaned toward Vanessa and whispered something in her ear. I gave Kyle a look. "Here these two lovebirds go again." I knew any minute Sean and Vanessa would step away from us. Boom. They did.

They went one car off from where we stood. Vanessa sat on this silver car's hood and Sean faced her. Almost standing between her legs. Nearly boy-friend-and-girlfriend close. They exchanged words, and she giggled and touched her hair.

At first, me and Kyle were stuck on stupid. Watching Sean. I started thinking about how he acted like his bad science grade was no big deal, but Kyle killed that. "Anyway," Kyle said, and jumped back into talking science. But while he spoke, my eyes kept going from him to eyeballing Sean and Vanessa. Finally, I stopped Kyle's blabbing.

"You think they together?"

Kyle shrugged. "Maybe." He kept speaking science.

I was probably annoying him because he was discussing school while I was talking nonsense, but my attention kept going back to Vanessa and Sean. They were in their own world. Kyle soft-punched me in my stomach. "You listening?!" he said.

"Why you hit me?"

"Look." His face got serious. "Me studying Sean

isn't going to help me get a good grade in science. You want to figure out our homework or what?"

"Yeah," I said.

Me and Kyle got 100 percent into talking science. Before we knew it, Sean and Vanessa came back over and we all bounced for home.

Thanksgiving break was four days long. Thursday, Friday, Saturday, and Sunday. Me, Sean, Vanessa, and Kyle usually saw each other during the break. This time it was different. Vanessa and her parents went and stayed with family on Staten Island. Kyle and his parents spent the break in Mount Vernon at his cousins' house. I missed hanging out with everybody, but the days went by fast.

Back in school, Sean didn't bring up his Thanksgiving in Philly. When I asked him about it, he said, "It was whatever."

The first weekend in December rolled around, and me, Sean, and Kyle slept over Kyle's. Around midnight Kyle was on his bed reading comics while Sean sat in a chair next to the window, playing a video game on his iPod Touch. I had just finished writing a new rhyme. "Guys," I said. "Listen."

"Whattup." They nodded.

I read fast in a tongue-twister way, like Eminem battle-rapping in that *8 Mile* movie:

I'm the magical, lyrical king of the hill.
With ill rap skills I spill.
I spray a new deadly style
Every different day while
I crush weak rappers, toss them in the junk pile.
See, you see me?
"Best MC." Today and forever in history.

Kyle just nodded and gave me a thumbs-up. His normal chill self and I expected that. But Sean stayed as quiet as Kyle. Totally unlike him. Normally, he'd rap back or tell me what was fire about my rhyme or how to make it better. Instead, Sean just smiled. "Cool," he said, and turned his video game back on.

Was Sean deaf? My rap was super-hot. What was he so serious for?

All night, Sean was as laid-back as Kyle. He smiled at my jokes but didn't crack any back. Later on, it felt like whenever I looked at him, Sean was either shut down and quiet or writing in his rhymebook. Twice, when he wrote, I grabbed my rhymebook and wrote too so I felt like me and him were doing the same thing.

Even Kyle acted worried about Sean. "He's mad quiet tonight," he said when Sean went to the bathroom.

"Right?" I said. But before we could talk more about it, Sean was back.

The next weekend, me and Kyle were supposed to sleep over Sean's place. Friday when we got dismissed from school, I looked for Sean so we could ride the bus home together. He was ghost. I thought I'd catch him at the bus stop on the corner of our school. Nope. Only Kyle was there. Vanessa wasn't meeting us. She had heard the girls' basketball team wanted new players so she had gone to after-school tryouts.

"Where's Sean?" Kyle asked me.

"I don't know."

Kyle looked away and mumbled, "He probably bounced on us again." He said that so quietly that it was like he was saying it to himself.

"What?"

"Nothing." Kyle turned back to me. "You try Sean's cell?"

I pulled mine out and tried, but Sean's voice-mail message came on. "No answer." I slipped my cell into my pants' pocket.

"Let's wait for him for five minutes, then go," Kyle said.

Soon, ten minutes passed and our bus pulled up. The doors opened and Kyle went to get on.

I stopped him. "Let's wait for Sean for a little longer."

"Why? You see him calling us?" Kyle said, annoyed. "Sean's having fun somewhere. Maybe he decided to take a later bus with his cousin Mark or another one of those seventh or eighth graders he's been hanging with."

What Kyle said about Sean maybe riding home with one of those kids sounded right. Sean was spending more and more time with them. Me and Kyle squeezed through the crowd of kids and went to the back of the bus. There, he put his iPod earphones in his ears.

On the ride home, I didn't bug Kyle about Sean anymore but I did try Sean's cell again. Twice. No answer. When me and Kyle got off the bus, we said if we didn't hear from Sean by eight o'clock, we'd do the sleepover anyway. At my apartment. When I got home, I rode my elevator upstairs and knocked on Sean's door. No answer.

At eight thirty that night, Kyle came over for our sleepover.

"Where you think Sean is?" I said.

Kyle breathed out heavy. "Maybe Jackie picked him up from school early. Took him to the movies or shopping until late. We'll hear from him later tonight or we'll see him tomorrow. Watch." Kyle stayed quiet for a few seconds. Was that his way of saying he didn't want to talk about Sean anymore? Did I sound like a scratched CD to him? Stuck on Sean? I switched the topic and asked Kyle if he had heard anything about Vanessa's tryouts. He hadn't.

About an hour later, Kyle was playing his hand-held video game. I got off e-mail and called Vanessa. "What happened with tryouts?" I asked her.

"I didn't make it," she said. "The coaches told me I need to work on my dribbling and layups."

Even though she said she was okay, she sounded upset.

"Next time, though," I said.

"Yeah," she said. "Next time."

Then I brought up the real reason I called. "You seen or heard from Sean?"

"Nope."

"He didn't ride the bus home with me and Kyle. We didn't even see him after school. Plus, nobody picks up his phones. Where you think Sean is?"

"Why you up his butt?" she said.

Me? Up Sean's butt? "Stop protecting your man," I said.

She laughed a fake laugh. Too hard to be real. "You still think I like him? I'm hanging up."

She did.

I was so heated that I slammed my phone in its receiver, then kicked the whole thing over.

Saturday afternoon, me and Kyle were on the handball courts in the stadium. As Kyle served the ball, he said, "Sean's ghost and I need to get my father's magazines."

Kyle had given Sean the latest *XXL* and *Vibe* yesterday morning before school. A thought popped into my head. If Sean had to give them back so fast, he wouldn't have time to write down rappers' rhymes for me. Then I realized my thought was dumb because Sean had stopped doing me that favor a while ago. He did that when we were close. Before his secret trips. I smacked the ball and wondered if Kyle really needed his pops's magazines back or if it was just Kyle's way of worrying about Sean.

"You just let Sean hold those magazines. Why you need them back so quick?"

"When I was getting my stuff ready for our sleepover, my father told me to get his magazines back. He didn't have a chance to read them yet."

Kyle underhanded the ball and roofed it over the wall by accident.

"I'll get it," he said, and jetted.

Over the weekend, I tried Sean again. His cell and house. No one picked up.

It was the same as the other weekends. Sean jetted. Only this time Sean hadn't lied ahead of time. He just bounced.

Monday morning at school Sean popped up in the second-floor hall as me, Kyle, and Vanessa walked to our first class of the day. Kyle acted as if Sean hadn't gone anywhere over the weekend. It was hard to front too, but I did and acted as if everything was normal.

The weekend before Christmas surprise, surprise . . . Sean vanished again.

This time, Jackie was in front of school at dismissal, waiting for Sean in a black livery cab with tinted windows.

"We seeing my aunt in Jersey." He fixed his black-on-black New York Yankees baseball cap and stepped in the cab and they drove off.

I didn't try calling him that weekend.

That Sunday night at bedtime I was only half tired.

My mind kept going from how close me and Sean used to be to how he'd switched up. I didn't know what to do with myself because I couldn't fall asleep. So I got my rhymebook and a black pen out of my backpack and sat at my desk. Sometimes I needed a beat to get my words going, but tonight I didn't need one. I opened my black-and-white Composition notebook and started writing:

I can't say much about how Sean switched up.

I thought we'd be tight from this day until we grew old and gray.

But it's strange how things change.

We don't even do things we used to.

Rhyming was our thing. Now, he rhymes with his new crew.

I wish I could wave a magic wand right now

And make me and Sean tight again right now.

But there's no magic, just reality

And Sean is vanishing. To where? That's a mystery.

Somebody knows his secrets, true?

What should I do?

Maybe stay up late one night soon

And catch him and his moms sneak off our stoop

And I'll yell from my window, "Where you both going to?"

But that's not right.

You don't disrespect your boy and his moms like that in real life.

I feel this can't go on.

If me and Sean don't go back to what we had all along,

Our friendship will be gone.

By the time I finished that last sentence, I felt more tired. My eyes were droopy. I shut my rhyme-book and slid into my bed and pulled the covers over my head. Right before I fell asleep, I thought I needed to do something about this Sean thing. Tomorrow. I'd talk to Vanessa or finally be up front with Sean.

Sean Strikes Out

MONDAY MORNING, me and Sean rode the bus to school together. On the ride, I wanted to ask him why him and his moms took so many trips. Who was on the bus that we knew from school? After a quick look, I didn't see anyone familiar. That made me less nervous. Every time I looked at Sean, I pumped myself up by saying stuff in my head like, "He's right here. Do it."

When this elementary school girl two seats from us got off the bus, it was just me and Sean in the back. Until that husky, white Dominican kid Manny with the green crossed eyes who liked messing with Sean in Friday Advisory came over.

"Punk," he mouthed at Sean, while standing pretty far away.

"Your father," Sean said, and gave him the middle finger.

Manny smiled, all evil, then turned and went to some of his friends.

With me and Sean now alone, I decided to try talking to Sean about his trips.

"Let me ask you a question," I said.

"Go ahead."

"I was watching television," I started, making up stuff as I spoke. "On *Maury* this guy said if your best friend lies to you, then he's not your best friend. You think that's true?"

"No."

"You ever lie to me?" I asked.

Sean squinted hard at something out the window, making his lying move. "You bugging. You know that? You my boy."

"So yes or no?" I asked.

"You gonna make us miss our stop, stupid." Sean got up and slipped into the crowd getting off the bus.

We walked to first period together, and I thought about being really honest with him then, but the timing felt off.

"I'm handing back your tests," our math teacher said.

At our table, she handed me and Sean mine and his.

"What you get?" I asked him.

"Sixty." When the teacher turned and walked away, he crumpled his test and stuffed it in his backpack.

I got a ninety and was about to show him, but I felt bad for him because a sixty-five is passing. I couldn't believe he failed another test. I wondered if I should drop confronting him about his trips, but by gym I didn't care about the perfect time to talk to him because he ignored me when we walked in. He went straight to his seventh- and eighth-grade friends. That got me heated. At the start of class, I sat on the floor and watched Mr. K take attendance. I looked at Vanessa. She was tying her sneakers.

I turned to Kyle and mouthed, "I need to speak with you. Don't play dodgeball."

"What?" Kyle mouthed back.

I made sure Sean wasn't watching me. He was busy joking with the kid behind him.

"Dodgeball." I moved my mouth more slowly. "Don't play dodgeball. Me and you need to talk."

This time, he got me and nodded.

"Free play!" Mr. K yelled.

Kyle and I headed straight for each other, but before we could talk, Sean ran up on us. "Where you going? You playing?" he asked, holding up the dodgeball.

I tried biting my tongue and thinking of an excuse for why me and Kyle needed to talk before playing dodgeball. But . . . the words flew out my mouth.

"Sean, how was Jersey?"

"Fine." He made his lying move.

"You probably went to Jersey this time," I said. Once I said those words, I felt more confident and everything next came out easy. "But that time you said your moms had friends over, you lied to me. She didn't have friends over. Me and Kyle stayed up late in my room. We saw you and your mother sneak out."

Sean just stood there. He looked at me, then at Kyle.

"So where you really went?" Kyle asked Sean.

Sean's face was surprised. Probably because he was used to Kyle minding his business.

Kyle's question shocked me too. I knew he was getting more and more tired of Sean lying, but I thought Kyle still would play the back role because he always wanted to respect people's privacy.

Sean's eyes went back and forth fast between me and Kyle. He was stuck on stupid and didn't know what to say.

"Tell the truth now," I said.

Instead, Sean made his lying face, shrugged, stared away, and said, "I don't even know what you two are talking about." He began walking over to the dodgeball area.

"Hold up," Kyle said, putting his hand on Sean's chest.

"Hold up nothing." Sean smacked Kyle's hand away. "You both called me a liar. I'm a liar then. I'm out."

Me and Kyle hesitated at first and just watched Sean leave. Then we followed him.

Two of Sean's eighth-grade friends wanted to play dodgeball with us again. Junito and Tony. In the middle of the game, Sean OD'd and pegged this boy Chris up close. None of the sixth graders threw the ball at Chris because he sometimes got into fistfights. He was like a ticking bomb. He exploded at the tiniest thing, and he wasn't afraid of Sean. He even flipped on kids who wanted to be his friend. That was why he had no friends.

Anyway, he was two feet from Sean when Sean gunned the ball at his head. That ball hit Chris's face so hard, his glasses flew off. The ball bounced back to our side.

"You out!" Sean said.

"Yo!" Chris yelled.

Sean picked up the ball and pitched it at Chris again. Chris tried turning away and the ball bounced off his shoulder.

"What?!" Sean yelled at Chris. "I'll hit you again!"

How come Sean was starting? And why with Chris? Chris wasn't a punk. He was a real fighter.

Chris rushed Sean and pressed his chest against him. He squinted, probably because he couldn't see Sean good without his glasses. Sean twisted his lips and looked at the ceiling like he was bored and wanted Chris to throw the first punch. "Hit me so I can knock your teeth out like your alcoholic father."

"Don't talk about my father," Chris huffed hard.

"Whatever!" Sean said. "Your drunk father, your drunk, dumb father, your bum, butt father."

Me and Kyle ran up and squeezed in between them.

Our gym teacher was nowhere to be found.

Sean's eighth-grade friends and a bunch of kids from the dodgeball game raced over too. Before I could tell Sean to chill, he mushed Chris's face. Chris's head snapped sideways. He got ready to hit Sean, but Sean's troublemaker friends jumped in.

"Touch Sean!" Junito shouted. "See what happens!"

"Hit Sean and I'll hit you!" Tony told Chris.

Everyone thought they were about to see a fight, if not between Sean and Chris then between Chris and Tony or Junito. Chris got into fights sometimes but he wasn't stupid. Tony and Junito were big eighth graders. If you saw them on the street, they could pass for high school kids. Tony was Mr. K's height, and I once heard Mr. K brag how he was six feet tall. If Chris fought Sean, Junito and Tony would jump Chris and turn his face into chopmeat.

Chris maybe got scared, because he walked off and shouted, "Where my glasses?"

Some girl handed them to him. He put them on and went toward the other side of the gym and disappeared into a crowd of kids at the volleyball area.

When Sean started to walk off with Tony and Junito toward the bleachers where the seventh and eighth graders were, I got close to him and grabbed his arm, soft. "You all right?"

He snatched his arm, hard, and snapped, "Leave me alone."

He walked off and the crowd of kids broke up and got back into dodgeball. Here and there, different kids said things like, "Did you see that?" and "Chris almost got jumped." It was just another school fight to them, but to me Sean mushing Chris was major. That was the closest I had ever seen Sean come to fighting.

When I looked at Kyle, he just shook his head.

Instead of playing we just kept watching Sean. When he got to the bleachers, Junito and Tony gave Sean pounds and slapped him on the back. Like he had just done something good by almost fighting. You could tell Sean's cousin was giving him props too. They surrounded him and cheese-grinned as if Sean were The Man. Sean seemed to enjoy that too much. He was so into it that he didn't catch Mr. K, a security guard, and Chris, the kid he mushed, quickly rolling up on him. Mr. K pushed into Sean's circle of friends.

"Sean, let's go!" Mr. K said. His eyes were mean slits. Him and the guard led both Chris and Sean away.

Sean was in trouble.

"Sean told me some things about fighting," I said to Kyle. "He said people fight when their feelings are hurt and that there are two ways of fighting: throwing hands and dissing. He said people who fistfight are dumb and can't use their words."

"So why did Sean almost fight right now?" Kyle said. "He could've beat Chris with words."

"Maybe something is bothering Sean and has his head messed up? Something from his last Saturday trip?"

Kyle pushed his glasses up his nose with his finger and crossed his arms. "Like?"

I was tired of trying to think about this with just Kyle. It didn't get us anywhere. I was ready to ask Vanessa questions. If she didn't know about Sean's secret Saturdays, then getting her involved was smart, because her plus me and Kyle meant three heads figuring things out. Three heads were better than two people playing detectives.

"Let's go talk to Vanessa."

"Bet."

Before, I was scared she'd run back and tell Sean we were spying on him. Plus, I was mad at her for hanging up on me. Now I didn't care. I knew Sean trusted her and she trusted him. Maybe Vanessa knew something we didn't. Or maybe she could find out.

Vanessa was on the other side of the gym shooting hoops with some girls. Our gym is maybe a block long and a block wide. It's so huge, crowded, and noisy that Vanessa couldn't have caught what had happened with Sean unless some kid had run over and told her.

"Vanessa!" I yelled. When she ran up to us, I started telling her what had happened. Kyle jumped in here and there. Our lips flapped fast like fans until we had told her everything.

"Wow!" she said real long. "Why didn't you come tell me first, before you played dodgeball with Sean?"

"Because," Kyle said. "We . . ."

". . . we don't know why," I said, finishing Kyle's sentence.

"Now what?" she asked.

"I don't know," I answered. "Maybe you can talk with him later?"

"Me?" She sounded surprised. "Why me?"

"Because he's feeling you," Kyle said. Hearing that from Kyle made me believe it for real because he said something about somebody only if he thought it was true.

As soon as Kyle said that, I checked for Vanessa's reaction. She didn't even blink. It was like she already knew Sean had feelings for her. I expected her to say "Ewww!" or be the way she'd been those times I'd mentioned Sean and her liking each other, but she wasn't.

"Justin, why you looking at me that way?" she asked me.

"Did you know Sean's been taking secret trips on weekends?" I asked her.

Kyle poked his glasses up his nose and waited for Vanessa to answer.

Her whole vibe changed. She wrinkled her face and said, "When?"

"A few times," Kyle said. "He missed our sleepovers and snuck out with Jackie late at night. We saw them."

"I didn't even know he missed any of your sleep-overs," she said.

I believed her. She sounded and looked surprised. "Yeah and he's been lying and saying he stays in Red Hook," I said. "But no one picks up his phones. Sean different with you?"

Vanessa shrugged. "No."

"He ever speak to you about something that made you worry about him?" Kyle asked.

She twisted her lip and looked like she was figuring out how much to tell us. "Justin, you and him had this Advisory together. Some guy came in and talking about loser fathers, right?"

"Yeah," I said.

"Sean told me about that," Vanessa said. "Sean said his dad was like that guy's pops."

"Really? What else he say about his father?" I asked.

"He said his dad had different sides to him and he hoped he never grew up to be like his father. After that, he never brought up his dad again."

"At least he still talks to you. He's been quiet around me and Kyle. Vanessa, I think if you spoke with Sean privately, you'd get a different reaction from him."

"This is bugged." Vanessa looked up at the ceiling.

"You could do it today in school or after," Kyle said.

I watched her try to make up her mind.

"I'm telling you he's changed because of those trips," I said. I wanted to say something else. Anything else to persuade her to help me and Kyle figure out what was happening with Sean. If she said no, me and Kyle had no other way of stepping to Sean. She had to say yes. I was desperate.

"Okay," Vanessa said real slow. Like she still wasn't sure if we were doing the right thing. "I'll do it."

Yes! Finally! She was down.

Sean didn't show up to class after second-period gym. He didn't come to fourth-period science either. In the hallway, when fifth period started, Vanessa came up to me and said, "I guess I'll have to call Sean after school. Stephanie from Class 601 was in the main office for using her cell in class. Anyway, she said she saw a security guard bring Sean in. Principal Negron called Sean's mother, and half an hour later, Jackie came up and took Sean home."

"What?" I said. "Is he suspended?"

"I don't know."

"Let's get Kyle. We need to see Principal Negron and find out what happened."

Going down the stairwell, we saw the back of my

Advisory teacher's dreadlocked head. I pulled Vanessa out of sight mad fast. The last thing we needed was Ms. Feeney turning around and spotting us on her way to supervising the cafeteria. She probably would've walked us to lunch and kept us there.

"I think she's gone," Vanessa said after about a minute of us sitting quietly on the steps.

When we got to the lunchroom, we found Kyle waiting for us outside the doors. He must've missed Ms. Feeney.

"We need to go to the principal's office," I said. "Jackie came in and took Sean home. He might be suspended."

Kyle's jaw dropped. He knew what I knew. Sean hadn't ever gotten into this much trouble before.

"Let's go," Vanessa said, grabbing Kyle's wrist because we didn't have time for him to be standing there with his mouth open.

As we headed to the principal's office, we passed Big Eddie, who said, "I heard Sean got suspended." He smiled. I was so pissed. I wanted to say something to him, but I couldn't think of anything. So I turned and gave him the middle finger.

When we got to the main office, we stopped at the counter.

It was the week before December break. Christmas

decorations were up everywhere. Gold and silver glittery garland was taped on walls in upside-down rainbows. Fake candy canes were stuck on windows.

But it didn't feel like Christmas was coming. The holidays were in the back of my mind. I was more focused on Sean's craziness.

The counter that blocked visitors from walking into the secretaries' area had swinging doors at both ends.

The plan was to rush through one of those swinging doors, fly past the three secretaries without them seeing us, and get to Principal Negron's open door. We checked on the secretaries. I couldn't completely see them, which meant they couldn't really see us. They had black computers on their desks with big, flat screens standing straight up like little walls. Their desk printers were tall and wide. Almost as huge as their desks. It was like they wanted to hide. They had to lean to the side to see people come into the office.

One secretary chatted with two lunch ladies. The second secretary spoke with a UPS man with packages. Two distracted secretaries meant we only needed to sneak by the third secretary, Ms. Dotson.

"You see Ms. Dotson?" Vanessa whispered at me and Kyle.

"Only the top of her head," Kyle said.

"Now then," Vanessa said. "Let's do this."

Me and Kyle nodded and we opened the swinging door closest to Ms. Dotson and snuck past her to Principal Negron's office.

We were almost at Principal Negron's open door when we heard, "Can I help you?" Ms. Dotson's head flew from behind her computer screen. She flashed a fake smile and asked, "Why are you three in here?"

We froze, but then Principal Negron walked out of the bathroom in his office wiping his half-wet hands with brown school bathroom paper and saw us. He pointed at me, straightened his tie, and started walking my way.

"Can I help you?" Ms. Dotson asked us again. Meaner. She probably didn't appreciate us not answering her.

"Ms. Dotson, it's okay," Principal Negron said. "Justin, Vanessa, and Kyle," he said real sweet. "Come in."

We followed him and stood near his long conference table. When he closed his wooden door, we all heard it click shut. My stomach growled from nervousness. His friendly grin made me more afraid. Usually, he was straight business.

There was this school rumor that Principal Negron used to be a police captain. I believed it. He had that mean cop walk, talk, and face. His mouth smiled but his eyes didn't. Both kids and teachers called his stare "the look." His stare was worse than getting yelled at or being asked a million questions. Whenever his eyes met mine, I felt like a criminal on a cop show on television. In a small, dark room under a hot lightbulb, being grilled.

He had an almost Santa Claus white beard. Instead of being big and puffy it was trimmed real close to his cheeks and chin. Little prickly white needles everywhere.

"Is it true Sean got suspended?" Vanessa asked him.

"Maybe I should ask Justin," Principal Negron said real calm. "Does Sean deserve to be suspended?"

"How would I know?" I asked.

Principal Negron looked at me suspiciously and crossed his arms. "Ms. Feeney tells me she sees Sean being mean a lot lately. Putting kids down so nastily, she'd almost call Sean a bully. And she says you're there when he does it. Is that right?"

I smiled but didn't know why I smiled. Maybe because I was nervous.

"Something's funny?" Principal Negron said.

"No," I answered fast.

"It better not be. If I see you acting like Sean . . . or if I see any of you putting kids down, I'll get your parents up here and you'll be suspended."

I knew Vanessa and Kyle's hearts were pounding like mine from what he had just said. Sean's mom was sometimes easy, sometimes hard. If she punished him, she sometimes got soft and let him do what he wanted. She'd tell him he couldn't be on the phone, then let him use his cell. She said no TV and video games but let him watch TV and play video games anyway. Other times, she was strict.

Our mothers didn't play that. They were always strict if we got into trouble. They hit us. Took away our privileges.

"I'm not going to speak to you like you're in kindergarten," Principal Negron said. "You three are getting older, right?"

We nodded.

"Do you know what's wrong with Sean making fun of kids?" he asked. His face looked as concerned as mine, Vanessa's, and Kyle's. Like he had Sean's back. "There are reports on my desk that all say the same thing. Putting someone down is verbal abuse. Kids who do this become adults who start verbal conflicts. Adults who verbally abuse are more likely to have problems with the law because they put the wrong person down and that person either responds with violence or they get the police involved.

"I told Sean and his mother where his nasty mouth might lead. If he keeps bullying now, he might grow into an adult bully and verbally assault people or more. She's upset about the trouble Sean's gotten into and says she'll turn Sean around. I hope she does, but he also needs your help. You're his best friends. Get him to cut it out."

"Okay," we all said at the same time. I could tell Principal Negron didn't want Sean to grow up to be a troublemaker.

"Go to lunch," Principal Negron said. "And I didn't suspend Sean out of the building. Tomorrow he's back and has in-house suspension."

As we left his office, I smiled a real smile. In-house was this room for kids who had done something bad but not so bad that they got suspended out the building and stayed home. There was still time for us to get to Sean and talk to him. Get him to stop bugging before he got suspended out the building for real because everybody knew what happened to kids who got suspended that way. They fell behind in school, would get in more trouble, their grades dropped, and soon they were left back.

Sean Is Day and Night

BY FOUR O'CLOCK, Sean hadn't called any of us. We went behind our building to shoot hoops on the court there.

Kyle took the ball and started doing layups. I whipped out my phone and dialed Sean's cell. It went straight to his voice mail on the first ring. I didn't leave a message. We played a game of Around the World. Then I played taps with Vanessa while Kyle dialed Sean's house. His mom picked up.

"Hello," Jackie said.

Kyle hung up.

"You hung up on her?" I asked Kyle. I was so into hearing his answer that I dropped the ball Vanessa threw to me.

"O-U-T," Vanessa told me. "You out."

"Yeah, I hung up," Kyle said. "I didn't know what else to do."

Sean's mom might've been annoyed that he'd put his hands on someone in school. She'd probably put her foot down and kept him from using his cell.

"Vanessa," I said. "Dial Sean's house on star 67." Star 67 is what you punch before a number if you don't want your number coming up on someone's caller ID.

Vanessa didn't want to bug Jackie because she liked her.

"Please," I asked her.

"Not for you," Vanessa said. "For Sean. I want to speak with him too." She star 67'd Sean's apartment.

"Kyle?" Jackie said. "Is this Kyle?"

Vanessa hung up. Her eyes popped out her head. "She thought I was Kyle."

"Dang!" Kyle said, punching his leg hard. "Now she's going to think it's me who keeps calling." He took his glasses off and rubbed the lenses with the bottom of his shirt.

We stopped calling Sean because it probably was just pissing his mom off. Maybe we'd see him tomorrow.

"Let's play a game," Vanessa said. "I'll start a sentence, toss the ball to one of you, and whoever gets it has to finish what I'm saying. Then you say that same sentence and toss the ball to somebody and we end it."

"Okay," I said.

Kyle nodded, still looking pissed about Vanessa hanging up on Sean's mom. "Whatever. Go ahead."

"Sean is fighting because . . ." She bounced the ball at me.

". . . because he stopped taking his pills that we never knew he took to control his anger." I repeated what she had said, "Sean's fighting because . . ." and passed the ball to Kyle.

". . . because he's dumb." Kyle threw the ball hard at Vanessa. "Sean's fighting because . . ."

". . . because he's turning into his father."

"You think?" I asked. That was really smart of her to say. I wanted to talk more about that but her cell rang.

"Hello?" she said. "Yes. Yeah. Okay." She hung up. "I'm leaving. My mom wants me home now."

"I should be out too," Kyle said.

We left the court and went in different directions, but what Vanessa said about Sean turning into his pops stayed on my mind for the whole night.

Both Tuesday and Wednesday passed and Sean never made it to school. His mom had pulled him out early on Monday. Now he was absent two days in a row? He was supposed to be in school serving in-house suspension. A scary thought ran through my mind. Maybe his mom kept him out because she was transferring him to another school. One where he wouldn't get into trouble. First, I felt that idea was dumb. But it wasn't. If Jackie took secret Saturday trips, she probably would make other moves on the sneak too.

Thursday night, I was alone in my room. With no Vanessa around to make me feel bad about calling Sean's house and hanging up, I tried Sean on his cell and house phones again. It was the same as the nights before. I star 67'd. Instead of Sean picking up, his mom answered, heard my silence, and hung up. A few times I almost spoke to ask Jackie what was up with Sean, but I couldn't. I was scared of how she'd react. Plus, she was grown, and my mother taught me to watch my mouth with adults. To respect. So I kept hanging up and after a while Jackie stopped answering. She probably turned her ringer off. I didn't blame her. I called so much that even I was hearing a phone ring in my head.

On Friday morning, I got to school at seven thirty, before first period. Kyle was in the cafeteria eating breakfast.

Sean sat on the other side of the lunchroom with his cousin Mark, Tony, Mike, and Junito.

"Let's go talk to Sean," I said.

"Nah. I'm curious about Sean but I'm mad hungry and I'm finishing my breakfast. Find me after at the table near the soda machine."

I went up to Sean alone.

"What up?" I said, and asked him to step to the side with me.

At a nearby lunch table, I took off my backpack, unzipped it, and pulled out my loose-leaf binder. I popped the rings and handed Sean the four assignments he had missed while he was gone.

"Where you been?" I asked.

"Nowhere."

"Anyway." I didn't feel like having a back-and-forth with him. "We still have forty-five minutes. I didn't do two assignments. Let's sit with Kyle and knock these out together so you can catch up before first period."

"Nah. I'm not doing the assignments."

Here I was hooking him up so he wouldn't fall behind. And he repaid me by dismissing me?

"Sean," I said, "why you gonna let your school-work slip?"

"Who cares if I hand in super-neat work, on time, all the time? That's corny. And nerdy."

Was Sean trying to impress his cousin and his eighth-grade friends? They never did schoolwork. "Okay," I said. "Fail and end up in summer school. See if I care."

"Bye then," Sean said, and walked back to his eighth-grade boys.

I couldn't believe Sean had just clowned me.

Sean stopped and looked back at me like he could feel me hating on him. "You want to come hang with us?"

Me? Flush myself down the toilet with them?

"Nah." I tapped my backpack. "I need to do these assignments."

I slung my book bag onto my shoulders and walked out the cafeteria into the courtyard, zipped up my coat, and sat on a concrete bench. I felt like hitting something. Even though it was cold out, mad kids ran around. Playing Chinese handball and tag, and jumping rope. One girl, getting chased by another girl, passed me and smiled. I smiled back but didn't feel smiley. I felt sick. Sick of how Sean had switched up on me. Sick of everything. It looked like my days of being tight with Sean were over.

I pulled out my binder to do my two incomplete assignments. Screw it. I shoved it back into my bag. Instead I yanked out my rhymebook and a pen, and started writing.

Since elementary, me and Sean been bugging
But just now, he saw me and didn't say nothing.
Ma says I should follow her advice and don't brush
it under the rug.

The way I feel is I can't stand it.
Me and Sean—we losing our friendship.

And Ma's advice is real because she speaks from
experience.
She caught my loser dad cheating with her best
friend, Jen.
And, finally, she confronted them.

She says it was the best thing she ever did
And she wished
She would've said something
Back when
My dad began flirting.
Instead, she kept her feelings in.
By the time she spoke up, she had lost her man and
her girlfriend.

So do I confront Sean? Or let him play me like a
fool?
I guess I got time to choose.

In the meantime, I'm not falling behind like him in school.

I closed my rhymebook. Feeling better, I decided to sit with Kyle in the cafeteria and finish my two incomplete assignments. Even if Sean didn't want to work on them or hang with me and Kyle. I didn't feel as angry with him as I had before but wasn't fully ready to throw away our friendship.

Fight! Fight! Fight!

ME AND SEAN WALKED TOGETHER INTO OUR LAST CLASS, Advisory. The same gang guy from before was standing with Ms. Feeney. Jay. The man with the messed-up family.

Me and Sean sat next to each other. So close our elbows touched. Sitting that way was how we sat as best friends. Maybe Sean did that to let me know we were still good. On the other hand, I didn't feel best-friend vibes between us. I bumped Sean with my elbow. He turned his eyes real slow to mine and looked dead into my grill.

"We should kick it after class," I said.

He nodded. "Yep," and smacked his lips on the *p*. Like Yep-puh! All obnoxious.

What he did that for?

Ms. Feeney made her peace sign and walked into the middle of the circle. Today, her outfit was fancier than normal. Dark brown suit, skirt plus blazer. Light pink blouse. Shiny high heels. Maybe she was going somewhere nice after work.

"Class, you remember today's guest speaker," Ms. Feeney said. "I think we need to hear what Jay has to say. Months ago, he was here but you interrupted him." She looked at Manny and Manny smiled, all devilish. Sean was clueless that Ms. Feeney stared at him too. He was leaned over, wiping a smudge off his brand-new white kicks. "Since then, Jay has been to schools all over the United States sharing his message. I invited him back for a second time and we're lucky his schedule allows him to visit us again. Please be more respectful this time."

Jay stepped into the circle. He was dressed again for work or church. "I just want to see how good your memories are. The last time, what did I start talking about?"

Manny snorted. "Family."

"Good," Jay said. "Let's pick up there."

Manny raised his hand and, out of nowhere, said, "Was your father gay? Boys with fruity fathers grow up to be fruity."

Jay and Ms. Feeney looked like they had plugged

their wet thumbs into electrical sockets and gotten zapped.

"W-what?" Jay stuttered.

"Was he fruity?" Manny said. "Like gay. Because Sean's dad's fruity and Sean came out fruity."

Everyone's eyes popped out. Even mine. We knew Manny was crazy and sometimes said wild things, but I couldn't believe what he had just said to our guest speaker.

"You have detention," Ms. Feeney snapped at Manny.

Manny shrugged and grinned. "I don't care. What I said is true."

"Manny, you the gay one," I said. "That's why you always riding Sean's jock and dissing him."

Sean raised his hand before I could say anything else and Ms. Feeney could slap me with a detention. "Can I go to the bathroom?" he asked real polite.

Ms. Feeney looked at Sean, proud. "Yes." I think she was happy Sean chose to leave the room instead of staying and dissing on Manny. Kids probably thought Sean was butt for bouncing and not beating up Manny with his words, but I was proud of Sean too. I didn't want him getting into trouble with Ms. Feeney.

Sean stood up and tugged at the bottom corners of his navy blue shirt. He made sure he was crisp. He brushed some lint off his shoulders and went to leave the circle. Manny was sitting right by the door. "Excuse me," Sean said nicely. Manny didn't move his leg to let Sean pass.

Out of nowhere, Sean punched Manny in the face. Hard! He rocked Manny with a left punch, then clocked him with a right. He just kept snuffing Manny and snuffing him. Manny grabbed Sean's waist and tried wrestling Sean to the ground, but Sean started dropping elbows on him.

Most of the class jumped up and pumped their fists, screaming, "Fight! Fight! Fight!" Some stood on their seats and shouted. A few kids were like me. Stuck on stupid. Shocked and watching.

The guest speaker and Ms. Feeney rushed Sean and Manny at the same time. Without realizing it, I got up to help too.

They pulled Manny one way and I yanked Sean in the opposite direction, but then Sean swung around and shoved me.

"Back up!" he yelled. "I'm good! I'm good."

He looked down and fixed his shirt. He examined his white kicks for marks. He found nothing there so he walked all hard toward the door.

"Sean! Get back here!" Ms. Feeney demanded.

Sean turned to see Manny holding his bloody

nose. Sean stuck his middle finger up at him, flung open the door, and left.

Ms. Feeney chased after Sean and popped her head out the door. "Security!" she yelled.

A security guard who was as fat as The Nutty Professor and as dark as a Snickers bar was down the hall, playing with his cell phone. The guard looked up at screaming Ms. Feeney, then at all-relaxed Sean.

"Take him to the principal's office," Ms. Feeney shouted. "His name is Sean and he just fought in my room."

"Come on, son," the guard said, all friendly, putting a hand on Sean's shoulder. Sean shook his hand off like a pit bull that didn't want to be chained.

"Don't touch me!" Sean barked. "I'll come. But don't touch me."

"Whatever." The guard held up his open hands in "I surrender" style. "Send me the other kid who fought," he told Ms. Feeney. She sent bloody Manny to catch up with Sean and the guard.

"Let's go," the guard said.

Sean pushed the swinging exit door open and him, the guard, and Manny disappeared into the stairwell.

Somebody patted me on the back and said, "Yo, your best friend laid Manny out." But all I could think was that the Sean who had just left wasn't my best friend. That was the new Sean. The old Sean never lied and never fought. This new Sean was a liar and let a dis faze him so much that he made Manny's nose bleed.

Dissing was about finding something wrong with someone and blowing up their spot. Did Manny find the right thing wrong with Sean? Because Sean had exploded. Was Sean gay? Was his father gay? Suddenly I realized something. Lately Sean's disses were almost always about kids' dads.

What happened with Sean and Manny got Ms. Feeney so angry, she grabbed a red Sharpie marker, pointed it at three trips on her wall calendar she had planned to take us on, and said, "Class, you see this trip, this one, and this one? They're all canceled." She X'd each one out. Most kids got mad because they couldn't wait to go on those trips. Big deal. I was thinking about Sean.

"After what I just saw here," Ms Feeney said, "forget trips and guest speakers. You want to jump on chairs, yelling, 'Fight, fight.'"

She called the names of the kids who had done that.

"You all have after-school detention today and we're calling your homes."

Then she made them get their loose-leaf binders and write two-page apology letters to the speaker.

"Make sure you explain what was wrong about what happened, how you should've behaved, and what's the right thing to do the next time you see a fight."

She complimented the few kids who hadn't done anything bad, then told the whole class to read for the rest of the period. Then Ms. Feeney and that gang guy sat at her desk and talked quietly for the rest of the time. About what? I couldn't hear and didn't care. Before his fight with Manny, I told Sean we needed to speak because I wanted me and him to get right with each other. I wanted to tell him I was angry at him but he was still my boy. That I still had his back. No matter what, I needed to show him that now.

Even Crazier

ADVISORY ENDED and I rushed to my homeroom class for my coat, then jetted to the main office. It was packed with kids and adults. The secretaries were busy giving bus cards to students and speaking with teachers.

I snuck past the busy secretaries to Principal Negron's office and peeked in. Sean and Manny were at his conference table. Principal Negron was yelling at them. His face wasn't sad for Sean anymore. It was hard-cop mean. Even more now that Principal Negron had shaved off his white beard. The only thing left was a white goatee that made him look like evil Santa. Sean and Manny had their arms crossed, and their tight faces looked at the floor. From the corner of his eye, Principal Negron spotted my head poking into his doorway.

"Justin!" he said. "Come in."

I walked in feeling dumb because he had busted me peeking. But at the same time I was happy too. Maybe I could talk to Principal Negron and get Sean out of trouble.

"Remember what I said the consequence was if something happened with Sean again?" Principal Negron asked me.

I nodded.

"Well, I just handed Manny and Sean suspensions for the week after Christmas break. Their parents are coming up to get them."

I talked fast. "Can I say something? It's not fair that Sean gets the same punishment as Manny. Manny disses on Sean every time we in Advisory. Plus, today, Manny started first."

Principal Negron smiled at me, half hard and half soft. I didn't know what that meant.

"Justin, you're absolutely right. That's where fights begin, don't they? With disses. So maybe I should double Sean's suspension?"

Sean looked at me like, "Stupid. Get out of here before you get me into more trouble."

"From what I've heard," Principal Negron continued, "Sean disses on kids a lot. Should I punish him for those times? You said it yourself. Fights start with disses."

I couldn't respond. Principal Negron was right.

"I like you, Justin. You stick up for your friends. But I told you I mean business, and I asked you in here to show you I do. You can leave now."

The hallway outside the main office was filled with loud students in coats, scarves, gloves, and hats. All flowing toward the exit doors. I joined the crowd and was soon outside with the cold air on my face. Kyle and Vanessa were on the sidewalk waiting for me.

"I heard," Vanessa said.

"How long he suspended?" Kyle asked.

We all started walking downhill to our bus stop.

"The whole week after break," I said. "I hope his mom doesn't OD and ground him for the break and the next week too. Then we might not speak to him for two weeks."

"Now what?" Vanessa asked.

"You should stop by his apartment to see him," I told her.

She bit her lip and thought it over. After two seconds, she said, "Even if his mom lets me in, I don't think Sean'll just tell me what's been going on."

"All this is because of his secret Saturday trips. I can feel it. Maybe he has things lying around that show where he's been. A bus ticket. A souvenir. If you see it, point it out. Say something like, 'Sean, where you go?' That might get him to open up."

Vanessa watched some boys play tag. One ran into the street and almost got hit by a car. The driver screeched to a stop, shot his head out, and yelled, "Animal!"

"You think Sean's bugging from his trips?" Vanessa asked me. "Maybe it's from something else. Like what Manny said. Sean only flipped on Manny when Manny joked on both Sean and his dad being fruity. Maybe they gay and we never knew."

"Yeah," Kyle said, changing his mind. "Maybe he lives in Puerto Rico with his gay boyfriend."

"Sean does stay getting little tiny, shiny things from his father," I said. "Grown men aren't into that. Females are. And gay guys probably."

Suddenly I wished me and Sean had talked more about his pops. I never pressed him about his because I didn't want to hear him brag when mine was a jerk. I knew one thing. When we were little, Sean never went to see his dad in Puerto Rico. And his pops didn't visit him. I didn't think anything of it because it was the same with me. I never went to see my father and he stayed ghost too. Maybe now Sean's mom had come into some money and started taking Sean to visit his pops in PR.

I snapped my fingers and said to Kyle, "Remember they had that suitcase? I wonder if Sean and Jackie went to the airport.

"Vanessa, you been to PR," I said. "Can you leave early Saturday and be back for school on Monday?"

"No doubt. When we flew there, it took two hours. You can go and be back in a day."

"Dang, son." I punched my fist into my palm. "Sean didn't tell us he was visiting him because he probably thought we'd ask questions." I paused. "None of Manny's other disses made Sean want to fight." I looked at Vanessa. "That's even more reason to pop up at Sean's. See if it's true."

Vanessa nodded. "Okay," she said. "But you think his dad really gets down like that?"

Vanessa Goes Spying

AT FIRST, I felt Vanessa spying in Sean's place was a good idea, but that night, the idea seemed wack. Why'd I even ask her to do that? If Sean busted her snooping, she probably would snitch and say I made her do it. I checked the digital clock on my dresser. It read 10 P.M.

"You missed it," Kyle said. "Didn't you?"

Kyle was on the floor playing Hunt or Be Hunted again. I was so busy picturing Sean busting Vanessa, I had missed Kyle zapping the biggest alien at the highest level. When I looked at the TV screen, a pile of ashes with two eyeballs blinked back at me. Kentucky Fried Alien.

"You think Vanessa is at Sean's?" I said.

"Most definitely," Kyle said. "She hasn't called. That means they together. Relax." Kyle pulled out a 50 Cent album from my stack of CDs and pointed at 50's pissed face. "This how you look. Calm down."

I rolled my eyes at him and restarted the video game. When I reached Level 2, my cell rang my favorite Black Bald song. It was Vanessa calling from her house phone.

"Hello?"

"You guys were right," Vanessa said. "Sean and his mom been breaking out."

"Kyle's here," I said. "I'm putting you on speakerphone." I was amped. Seven hours ago, Sean had gotten suspended. Since then, Vanessa had found out something. Crazy fast.

"Go ahead."

"When I went to Sean's apartment, his mom was happy I came because I brought Sean's schoolwork for our break. His mother said his teachers didn't make a homework packet for him."

"Good move with the homework idea," Kyle said.

"Thanks. Jackie pointed me to Sean's room. I knocked and he rushed me in, slamming his door hard like him and his mom were beefing. I said why I came. When he sat at his computer, I saw these CDs on his desk. Underneath them an envelope stuck half-way out. 'I LOVE YOU, SEAN' was written everywhere on it in different colored pens. Red. Green. Blue. Letters so big I saw them from where I stood. Whoever wrote that really wanted Sean knowing they loved him. Anyway, Sean's mom all of sudden yelled for him. He flung his door open and said all mean, 'What?' Jackie shouted back, 'Keep talking back to me and watch you get nothing for Christmas.'

"Sean went into the living room and slammed the door behind him. Maybe he did that so I couldn't hear them arguing. But I heard them shouting through the door. She's pissed at how he's behaved in school lately. Anyway, I rushed and looked under that stack of CDs. The envelope had a Polaroid stuck to it."

"Was it a picture of Sean's dad with his gay boyfriend?" I asked.

"No!" Vanessa said, disgusted with me. "Sean's father definitely was in the picture, though. The Polaroid had writing in blue ink at the bottom saying, 'Thanks, Sean, for the visits. When I'm home, I'll show you the type of dad I can be.' And Sean's father didn't seem gay. He looked thug. His face was harder than Principal Negron's. He had a baldie cut and rocked a wifebeater with green pants. Around him were diesel dudes just as gangster as him. They wore green pants too. I couldn't read where the envelope came from because the address was torn off when it was opened. Only two words were left. Clinton Co. That's it."

I heard Vanessa's mom say, "End that call. It's almost time for you to go to bed."

"I need to go," Vanessa said, then paused. "Another thing. I . . . I . . . I think I did something stupid."

"What?" me and Kyle said at the same time.

I felt my heart thump hard in my chest.

"Sean's rhymebooks were under a stack of textbooks. From how it was under all that, I thought he hadn't written in it in a while. So . . ." Vanessa stopped speaking and was quiet for two seconds like she thought about not finishing her sentence.

"So what?" Kyle asked.

"I grabbed one of his rhymebooks and stuffed it in my bookbag," she said fast and nervous. "I have it right now. That was dumb, right? You think he'll miss it? I don't think he'll miss it. I mean it was buried under all that stuff. Then again . . ."

"Nah," I said real slow to calm her. "Nah. It wasn't stupid. We got his thoughts right there. He might've written what's going on with him. We don't have a lot of time with that book, though. Bring it over first thing tomorrow. Let's read it, then sneak it back into his room." I was trying to sound confident and convince Vanessa that grabbing his book wasn't stupid. But yo! She was dumb for doing that. I mean, she might be right. Sean probably wasn't writing lately. But still! I didn't want to risk us holding his rhymebook for too long.

"End that call," Vanessa's mom said again.

"I need to go."

"What you think is in Sean's rhymebook?" Kyle asked, slumping back in his chair. "I can't believe she took it. How's he not going to miss that?"

All I could think was that we had Sean's rhymes! We could figure this all out! That was more than I had wanted her to find.

"We really going to read his rhymebook?" Kyle asked.

"No doubt," I said.

"This is crazy." Kyle ejected his video game and grabbed his hoodie. "Tomorrow then."

"Peace."

Two Criminals and a Short Convict

THE NEXT MORNING, I PHONED SEAN'S HOUSE AT NINE.

"Hello?" Sean's mom answered.

"Hi, it's Justin." Christmas music was playing in her apartment. "Rudolph the Red-Nosed Reindeer."

"You not calling to ask if Sean can hang out, right?"

"No," I said.

"Good. Because he's on punishment. And he's not getting on the phone." She sounded heated. "He's not coming out either."

"Okay."

She got quiet for a second. "Justin. Can I ask you something?"

"Yeah?"

"Where were you when Sean was getting into all this? You're his best friend. You should've stopped him."

I didn't know if I could sit on the phone and listen to her blame me when it was her fault Sean flipped. I wanted to tell her off.

"Me stop him?" I thought about saying. "Here are some things I did to stop him. First, I tried stopping him when he wilded out in gym. Second, in Advisory, I pulled him off Manny when they fought. No other kid did. Third, I went to the principal and tried to get Sean out of suspension. Fourth, I even brought Sean his homework so he wouldn't fall behind. So don't blame me. It's your fault Sean's in trouble. You taking him to Clinton Co . . . whatever. That place is messing him up." But I didn't have the guts to say those things to her because she's grown. Instead, I agreed with her and we hung up.

But then I thought maybe I should have done more to help Sean. I just didn't know what else I could've done.

Two hours later, Kyle and Vanessa showed up at my house. Ma was napping in her room. Vanessa didn't even sit. She pulled Sean's rhymebook right out and handed it to me.

I felt like I had Sean's life in the palm of my hand.

It felt good, but it didn't feel right. We were about to go through Sean's private thoughts. I had this feeling maybe we shouldn't do it but decided to go ahead with reading Sean's raps anyway. I needed to know what was going on.

"Did you look in it yet?" I asked Vanessa.

"No. I felt weird. Maybe we shouldn't even read it now."

"Whatever." I opened the book. Vanessa and Kyle slung their coats on my bed and sat on either side of me. For a split second, I had the same feeling in my stomach as when Sean dared me to go into the Grey House.

"I wonder if there's a rap in here about us," I said. I started flipping through pages fast. Sean didn't have dates on his rhymes, which made it hard to find the ones about his Saturday trips. I put dates on all my raps. Just to make sure my rhymes stayed fresh and I didn't rap the same way I had the month before.

I came to a page with lyrics about Sean's mom. I scanned the verses and caught a line saying, "She takes good care of me," and kept reading. But it was only some rap he wrote about his mom treating him nice.

I kept turning pages. I spotted a title. "Two-Faced." My eyes zipped up and down the page. Bam. I read Sean's words out loud.

I haven't spoken to no one about these trips.

And it makes me sick,

Seeing my dad ill like this,

Then coming back to my friends

And keeping Dad's secret from them.

I haven't done a sleepover in a minute.

Ma made me skip the one around Thanksgiving.

I bet she'll make me miss the one around
Christmas too.

And all my lies to Justin are weak but I don't know
what to do.

Justin spots stuff quick and I have to lie mad fast.

Like the time he went in my drawer and found that
cash.

I told him it's Puerto Rico dough my pops be
sending.

But it's really money that I don't be spending.

I add that to Ma's money so she can buy my dad
some things.

I don't do it for my dad. I do it for Ma. It feels good
helping.

I'm supposed to tell my dogs about stuff going on.

But how can I tell them now?

They'll be like, "Why you kept so quiet so long?"

I clown kids about their wack daddies.
So what would heads think
If they realized the one with the ill dad was me?

I think I can trust Justin.
I mean . . .
He won't make fun.
Then again I rather die before I tell anyone.
What about Vanessa? I think she'd be cool.
Then again, she's a girl and girls do the most
gossiping in school.
I could tell Kyle but then again I don't know.
Maybe it's best if none of them know.

Dealing with this drama is a daily headache.
I told my moms my feelings and she said, "Telling
anyone is a big mistake."

The rhyme ended. Wow! I knew Sean was hiding a secret and it had to do with his father.

"Find another rap!" Vanessa nudged my side.

I flipped the page and scanned. Nothing. I flipped again. A title said "Justin."

"This one's about you," Kyle said, and bumped his elbow against mine. All thirsty, he started reading the rhyme to us before I had a chance to check the verses for disses on me.

> *Justin wants to play detective*
> *Like he's a cop.*
> *Every time he sees me he asks me nonstop,*
> *"Sean, where you went this weekend?"*
> *What's up with his questions?*
> *Like he's my girlfriend*
> *Why he on my butt?*
> *Why he cares?*
> *I don't ask him, "Why's your dad not here?"*
> *Or, "How come you on welfare?"*
>
> *Justin should just stop.*
> *It all started after the first time I visited my pops.*

I wanted to take Sean's rhymebook and rip it in half. He said I was on him like I was his girlfriend. Dang, son. How come he had to write that in his book? What if Sean had another, even more hard-core verse on me?

"Give me that," Vanessa said, grabbing Sean's book from Kyle. She searched for another important rhyme. She found it. Sean called it "Let the Hands Do the Talking."

I've been ready to hit Manny

Way before today.

I've been feeling this way about fools

Almost every day since pre-K.

Because every day, since then, some kid tries to
play me.

Big respect to the advice Ma gave me.

She meant good by saying I should slay bullies with
words

And for a long time, I have, and I've made these
clowns look absurd.

But with a dis, people try to dis back,

But a hater can't say jack

If you knock him out and lay him flat on his back.

That's why I mushed that kid in gym

When he got loud with me.

And it's why I clocked Manny.

To tell the truth, when I saw Manny's bloody nose, I
felt bad,

But scrap that.

He mentioned my dad.

Manny could talk about anybody in my family but
not my pops.

God, when I think about my father,

It makes me so mad I want to pop.
And I've dropped
In my grades
And in my attendance.
Every day I'm late.
Why? Ma doesn't care so neither do I.
She only cares about taking me on these trips.
So forget about me handing in work that's crisp.
Ma doesn't care about me so I don't care about my
academics.

"Yo!" Kyle said. "He just wrote this rhyme. That fight with Manny just happened."

Vanessa shoved me. "See? I told you I was stupid to take this book."

I shook my head at Vanessa. "It just means you need to return this book real quick. That's it. He won't know it was gone. Watch."

Her face was mad tense. I didn't think she believed me.

I flipped backward to a few pages before and found a rhyme called "Ma."

We read it quietly.

Ma tried testing me.
I didn't straighten my room so she started
stressing me.

She said, "Keep it messy and we won't see
your dad."
Please! If I didn't see him, I'd be glad.
These trips are for her. During our visits, they both
ignore me.
I told Ma, "Let's stop seeing him. See if I care."
She's all talk, no action.
I didn't clean my room and she still brought me back
there.

I tell Justin, Vanessa, and Kyle that me and my dad
are close, but it's not true.
I keep lying because I don't want them to see I don't
have a perfect family.
But dang. My parents ain't even married.

On one trip, I told Ma, "We never visited him
before. Why now? Why bother?"
She said, "I feel more strongly now that boys also
need their fathers."
Plus, she said that before, I was younger, but now
I'm ready since I'm older.

"Wow!" Kyle said real long. "This explains a lot."
We went through the rest of Sean's book, but
there was nothing else about his father or the trips.

Vanessa jumped in. "Whatever's happening with his dad did make Sean flip. Sounds like he doesn't even want to follow his mom's advice no more. Now what?"

I looked at Vanessa holding Sean's rhymebook. "You need to sneak that back into the pile where you got it from as soon as possible."

"How?" Kyle asked. "She can't say she bringing him homework again. She used that excuse already."

Then, Vanessa bit her lip and thought.

"You bringing it back?" I asked.

Then Vanessa's face lit up and she smiled like she'd found money. "Yep. Right now."

"How?" Kyle asked.

"Don't worry." She got up, grabbed her coat, and headed for the door. "I got this."

Vanessa had bounced an hour ago. Not hearing from her made me a little nervous.

"Vanessa'll probably call in a minute," Kyle said. He was at my CD player looking for music to put on.

"Yeah," I said.

I took my cell out of my pocket and checked for missed calls. Maybe Vanessa had tried me but my cell hadn't rung. Nope.

Kyle picked an Old School joint to play. It was those two rappers who used to wear big, thick rope gold chains. The beat was hot.

"Turn the volume up," I said.

"You think Vanessa could do it?" Kyle asked, twisting the dial and making the music louder.

"I don't know. She tricked Sean once. I hope she can do it twice."

Suddenly, my cell sang my favorite hip-hop song. Kyle quickly lowered the music. The caller ID glowed bright red, "VANESSA." I scooped it up.

"Hello?"

"Done," Vanessa said.

"Word?"

"Never doubt me. I went to Sean's and asked him if I'd left my cell in his house. I turned my cell off in case Sean said, 'Let's call your cell and wherever it rings, there it is.' I'm glad I did, because that was the first thing he said. When he didn't hear anything, I said, 'I think I left it in your room.'

"His mom wasn't there. She had gone to the store. So me and him looked almost everywhere in his room. Finally, he said what I was wishing he would say. 'Vanessa, let me check the living room. You was in there talking with my mom before you came into my room, right?' So Sean went into the living room. That's when I snuck his rhymebook back mad fast into that pile. Guess what."

"What?"

"He didn't miss it because those textbooks were

in the same place. Same positions. When Sean came back into his room, I stood there holding my cell and said, 'Found it. It was under your beanbag.' And he believed me because it was the one spot we didn't check."

"Nice. Where you at now?" I asked.

"My place. I'll catch you tomorrow. I'm going to the movies with my mom."

"All right. Tomorrow."

"You know," Vanessa said, "it would've been a wrap if he'd caught me."

"Yeah."

"You and Kyle owe me."

"For real."

I closed my cell. "She did it."

Vanessa gave us what Sean was thinking but not saying. Still, there were some things we needed to know. Like in Sean's raps, what was "the place" Sean's dad was in? And why was his dad ill? Was he ill, sick? Ill, in a messed-up situation?

Kyle got hyped probably for the same reason I was happy. We didn't need to deal with Sean knowing we took his book.

Kyle turned up my radio and rapped to that Old School song.

"Make it louder." I jumped in and beatboxed.

• • •

On Christmas morning I woke up, hyped, and ran in the living room to open my gifts. Ma always got up before me, put on Christmas music, and made breakfast. She sat on the sofa, waiting for me. The smell of her pancakes, eggs, and sausages had our whole apartment smelling good. Ma worked hard for days hooking up our Christmas tree. It was covered in rainbow-colored lights that blinked on and off. Shiny bells hung from every branch. Different-sized gifts were wrapped real neat with bows on them and stacked on the floor underneath. I didn't know what to open first.

"Ma, which gift should I start with?"

"You choose." Ma smiled back at me. But she was rubbing and massaging her leg, so I knew she was hurt even though she was trying to look happy. It pissed me off that she had to be in pain on Christmas.

I picked up a square package and read Ma's handwriting. "To my Little Man, Stick with it and you might become famous for your words. Love, Ma."

I tore off the wrapping. It was a brand-new rhyme book. One hundred times nicer than the one I had. Soft brown leather with gold corners. Good, crisp, thick paper inside. It looked like it should belong to a rich person.

"Ma, this is cool." I wondered how much it cost.

"I thought you'd like it." She winked.

I kept opening gift after gift until nothing was left. I got most of what I wanted, but not some other expensive stuff I fiended for. Like an iPhone or a new video game system. I didn't beef. Ma looked at me like she hoped I was happy. I bum-rushed her with mad kisses and she started laughing and crying a little.

After Ma stopped crying, we ate breakfast and she told me the same old funny stories of Christmases from when she was growing up. Then I took my empty gift boxes and ripped wrapping papers to the garbage chute to help keep the apartment clean for Ma.

Christmas calmed my projects down. Less drama on the streets and even rude, troublemaking kids smiled and said hi to old folks. In our buildings, halls had less heads hanging out. Holiday songs played from behind doors. People were more peaceful but not cleaner.

Near the trash chute there was a humongous pile of crumpled gift-wrapping papers and mad empty toy boxes. The chute door was wide open with a full bag of garbage sticking out. Some nasty neighbor didn't shove their Christmas morning trash all the way down the chute. Seeing that made me feel like tossing my junk on the messy floor like them, but Ma taught me better. I pushed whoever's garbage down. Something wet leaked on my hands. I smelled it. Sour milk mixed with something that looked and smelled like baby poop. Dang, I hated inconsiderate people. I cursed in my head and rammed my garbage into the incinerator. Pissed.

Later in the day, me, Vanessa, and Kyle were supposed to meet at Kyle's to see what presents we got.

At twelve o'clock, I knocked on Kyle's door. While I waited for him to answer, this kid Omar who lived next door came out of his apartment with a man who had his arm wrapped around Omar's shoulders. The dude had Omar's same-shaped face and everything, so I guessed it was his pops. Every now and then, usually holidays, birthdays, or for graduations, fathers of kids in Red Hook would suddenly pop up. These dads be gone all year and then they come out of nowhere. I figured that was why Omar had a stank face on. Who wants a father once a year? Kyle opened his door right as Omar and his dad passed by me.

"You got good stuff?" Kyle asked.

"Yeah," I said, lifting my shopping bag. "It's in here. Vanessa show up?"

"Ten minutes ago." In Kyle's room, Vanessa was at his TV, messing with his DVD player.

She stood to say what up to me and a new gold chain with her name on it swung on her neck.

"Ouch," I said, covering my eyes. "Watch your bling. It's blinding me."

"Stop being stupid." Vanessa laughed. She showed

me her other gifts. A nice coat and a DVD box set of AND 1 basketball games. That was what she was messing with when I came in. "What you guys get?"

"This new skateboard," Kyle said, grabbing it off the floor. "I already showed Vanessa that. But she hasn't seen this." Kyle went to his closet, opened it slowly, and said, "Wait for it, wait for it. . . . Bam! This Rock Band game!"

"Son, we need to play that," I said, pulling my gifts out my bag, fast. "I got this new hip-hop CD, this rhyme book, two new Tech Decks with a half-pipe ramp." I pointed to my kicks. "And these sneakers."

"Oh snap!" Vanessa said, grabbing my CD. "Burn me a copy."

"All right," I said.

"Let me see that Tech Deck," Kyle said, taking one. "I'll teach you this new flip and some grinds I just learned. Oh, Vanessa, you want to still play that DVD?"

"Yeah," she said. "Both of you, sit down and watch this. Yo, see how this one girl from Harlem dribbles! I'm going to learn how to play like her. Then the coaches of the girls' basketball team will sweat me at the next tryouts."

We ended up watching Vanessa's b-ball DVD for thirty minutes. Just when I got tired of watching this dunking contest, Vanessa said, "You guys think we should call Sean?"

I was glad she suggested it.

"Yeah," Kyle said. "It feels weird without him."

I guessed they stayed thinking about him too.

We crowded around Kyle's bedroom phone.

"Okay," Kyle said. "Say Merry Christmas, then our names, on the count of three. One, two—"

"Wait," Vanessa said. "Kyle, you say your name first, I go second, then Justin."

"Fine," me and Kyle said.

Sean's voice mail picked up after one ring. Kyle counted us off and we yelled, "Merry Christmas!" into the phone. "It's us, Sean. Kyle, Vanessa, and Justin."

That felt good.

Then the three of us started playing Rock Band. We played until it was time for me and Vanessa to go home.

New Year's Eve, around seven o'clock at night, Ma sent me to the store. New Year's in Red Hook was the opposite of Christmas. Heads wilded, and outside, firecrackers exploded everywhere. The halls were extra crowded on every floor with people smoking weed, drinking, rolling dice, and messing up everything. Half the guys I saw, I didn't know. Some of them were there to start trouble because that was as much fun to them as getting high or drunk.

"What's your name?" this one kid maybe two, three years older than me asked when I passed through a crowd on the second floor. "You look mad familiar." He stepped toward me, and his crew of boys stopped laughing with each other to eye me.

"What's your name?" I said back, hard. If he thought I was soft and I gave up my name easy, then what else would he try to make me give up easy? My money? Or worse, if his boys thought I was a punk, they might try jumping me. "I've lived in this building forever," I told him, "and you don't look familiar."

He just stood there looking at me for a second like he was thinking about what to do next. Then, out of nowhere, Glenn from the fifth floor stepped forward to give me a pound. "Yo, Justin, what's good." He turned to his homeboy. "Chill. He's all right."

The guys, one by one, nodded what up to me then and slowly went back to joking with each other. I left for the store.

Every year, on this day, I had to deal with or see drama. That's how come me, Kyle, and Vanessa didn't hang on New Year's Eve. Going straight to the store and back was one thing, but us walking through different blocks to visit each other wasn't so safe. Sometimes, Sean and me chilled. Only because we lived in the same building and walking from floor to floor was safer.

On New Year's Eve, right before midnight, there were a bunch of gunshots out my window. Drug dealers blasted to celebrate. While they did that, me, my mother, and people in their apartments banged pots and blew horns. Then, at exactly twelve o'clock, the guys busting guns, me and Ma, and all of Red Hook yelled the same thing over and over: "Happy New Year!"

The day after, me, Vanessa, and Kyle promised to meet at my place to try and figure out more about where Sean's father was.

As soon as Vanessa walked in, she jumped on the Internet and said, "Let's Google the words *Clinton Co.*"

"Oh snap!" Kyle said. "How dumb were we for not doing this sooner?"

We stood behind Vanessa and a few seconds later mad stuff about Clinton County popped up on the screen. Some sites had words so big we needed a teacher to even say them. Vanessa clicked on one thing and people in business suits showed up. She kept hitting any link with Clinton in it. But none of the sites had anybody in it who even looked like me, Sean, Vanessa, Kyle, or Sean's father.

"Mmm." Vanessa said to herself.

"We could be doing this forever," Kyle said.

"For real," I said.

Me, Vanessa, and Kyle still didn't know what the words on the envelope meant and we agreed we couldn't just ask anyone. What if it was a bad place? We might've gotten in trouble.

After a couple more minutes of randomly clicking and finding nothing, we all were frustrated and quit.

We were back in school before we knew it. Walking through the halls on Monday without Sean cracking jokes felt weird. But by Wednesday, it was kind of nice not seeing him dis kids and make them deflate. I still missed him, even though he still hadn't called any of us. But that also meant he didn't know we took his rhymebook. Believe me, if he knew, we would've heard from him.

Friday, Advisory came.

When I walked into class, three grown thug guys stood in the circle with Ms. Feeney. They looked scary but familiar. Two were giants and built like wrestlers. One wore a do-rag. The other had a cheese grin on, a gold front, and a green hoodie. The third guy was short. Almost my height. But he was diesel too. He had frizzy cornrows. I glanced at them like "I'll be way over here. Nowhere near you."

The giant with the gold front must've caught my reaction.

"Little man," he said to me. "Come sit over here. I

won't eat you." He laughed like he was lying about that.

Was he trying to play me? He shouldn't play me, he should play lotto. I sat in the chair right next to him. He smiled at me. I nodded hard at him like I wasn't a punk.

"Attention, class," Ms. Feeney said. "To welcome you all back from winter recess, I have a special Friday Advisory for you. Today, we have three guest speakers instead of one. Each man here did jail time. They'll tell you how it was."

Before the break, Ms. Feeney had said no more speakers for my class because of Sean's fight with Manny. I guess she had changed her mind.

"I'm Davon," the giant with the do-rag said. His voice boomed and bumped like a car speaker. "Raise your hand if you been in a prison."

Nobody raised their hand.

Suddenly he barked, "Raise your hand when I speak to you! Raise 'em!" I jumped. Everybody jumped. Even Ms. Feeney.

That's when it hit me. I knew these guys from TV! These three dudes were on this ABC show. They went from school to school scaring kids into behaving. To keep kids from ending up in jail.

The gold-toothed giant with the hoodie said, "My

name's Reese. Ms. Feeney told me you had a fight in this room." He switched his voice to whiny. Teasing us. "She said you acted like little monkeys yelling, 'Fight! Fight!'"

Kids made faces like Ms. Feeney was a liar.

"You think fights are funny?" Reese barked at one kid smirking next to him.

"No," the kid said, and shook his head real fast.

The giant started undressing! He took his hoodie off until he wore a wifebeater. We watched him, wondering what was wrong with him.

Because he had just a tank top on, I could see he had a scar like a brown snake going from his throat to his shoulder and down to his forearm. Reese breathed in deep like a monster that ate scared kids. "See this?" he said all soft, and showed his scar to some kids.

They nodded.

"It's from fighting!" he shouted at them. "I can't even use my arm good! You think that's funny?

"My housing project was no joke. Traps everywhere. I don't mean fake trapdoors like you see in movies. I mean real-life traps. Drugs. Fast money. All types of things that'll kill you. Kill your future. Me and my brothers made the wrong moves. Fell in them traps. That's why we all did jail time. I'm not talking about these cats up here. I'm saying me and my real blood brothers did bids."

Davon, the other giant rocking the do-rag, said, "Me and the guys you see up here, we could've done different. Could've been different. But we was taking shortcuts. Following the easy road. With everything. I wasn't real with school. I wasn't real with my friends. I wasn't real with my girlfriends. Here and there, older people who did right tried talking sense to me.

"One time, I'll never forget. I was a junior high student and one friend told me he'd be in college someday. I laughed and called him a nerd. So bust it, that same year we was in his apartment and his father, out of nowhere, gave us this quick lecture. 'Don't cut corners,' he said. 'The corners you cut might come back and cut you.'

"He meant stay in school, be our best around everybody. To me, that was garbage. Why? I admired Gs, thugs. In my mind, him and any older, do-right dudes in my neighborhood were soft. So I didn't follow his advice.

"I kept going the wrong way, chasing fun.

"If it was easy, I did it.

"If it was hard, I didn't do it.

"I should've listened to my friend's pops. My friend didn't cut corners. Guess what. He ended up in college. And me? Just like his father said.

"I dropped out of school, and with no degrees I couldn't get work. I was shady with my friends and backstabbed some of them too. They stopped trusting me. Stopped looking out for me. One guy I was really foul with called the police on me when I started selling drugs. That's how I first got locked up."

The short guy with the frizzy cornrows jumped in and said, "My name is Mystic. In jail, guys doing bids look like the thugs you respected in the street. In prison, some of them even got a little juice. They run this or that. You see them and you say to yourself, 'Oh, he's The Man.'

"But how you a man if you in jail? How you a man when your children are out in the world and they need their father but you far away and can't be a dad? You can't put food on your children's table. You can't protect them. Some things only a dad can teach, but you gone, and you lose that chance. Your kids gotta get their life lessons from wherever they can. You ain't no man in jail. Every day prison guards treat you like a child. You need a cop's permission to use the bathroom. They tell you when to eat, wake up, sleep. In jail, I got older and grew. Soon, I looked like a man but still I wasn't a man. Why? Every day, I was handled like a caged animal. And when they let me out of jail, what did I know? The same stuff I knew when I first got sent to jail. I was a stranger to my kids and I had no real job skills. So I went right back to doing what was familiar to me as a kid."

Mystic got quiet. His face looked sad. "Don't ever get locked up." He slapped his hand to his chest. "Do me that favor. If you go to jail, the traps there can kill you or break your spirit. The guards . . . they take your clothes. Your style. Make you wear these green uniforms. In some jails, it's orange jumpsuits or . . ."

Green uniforms. Green pants! Vanessa said Sean's dad wore green pants in the Polaroid. I suddenly wanted to ask the short guy a question and raised my hand without realizing it.

"Whattup, shorty?" Mystic said.

"Did you wear green pants?" I asked.

Davon, the giant with the do-rag, smiled at me. What was he smiling at me for?

The short guy, Mystic, took one finger and tapped it to his cornrowed head. "Yeah. The people who run jails mess with inmates' minds. They make you feel like you have no identity. They take away your name and give you a number. You have to rock the same prison uniform as everybody else. In our jail, it was green."

"What jail were you in?" this boy Dennis asked.

"I was in a joint upstate," Davon, the do-ragged giant, answered. "The Clinton Correctional Facility."

My eyes almost flew out my head.

Clinton Co. I remembered the words that Vanessa saw on the envelope from Sean's dad: "Clinton Co."

Was Sean's pops in jail right here in New York? Was that "the place" Sean mentioned in his raps? How long had Sean been lying to me about his father? Before his secret Saturdays, I thought me and Sean knew everything about each other. Before those trips, I considered Sean my family. Now, these guys from jail were adding pieces to the Sean puzzle and I didn't know which way was up. Was Sean ever real with me?

I only half listened for the rest of Advisory.

When Advisory ended, all the students were almost out Ms. Feeney's door, but I stayed. I wanted to talk with the giant with the do-rag.

I felt uncomfortable, but Ms. Feeney was in the room so I knew it was cool to speak with him. I peeped his two friends chatting near the windows.

"Excuse me, Davon."

"Whattup, shorty?" he asked me.

"Can I speak to you for a second?"

He nodded.

I wondered how to start. Something told me that he knew Sean's father. "One of the kids that fought in here was my boy Sean," I said. "Did you know his dad? You were in the same jail as him. Clinton."

Davon's voice dropped mad levels, all friendly. "Yeah. How come Sean threw hands?" He said Sean's name like he knew him.

"The other kid clowned him," I said. "He called Sean's father fruity."

"Fruity?" Davon laughed. "Bro, you haven't met Sean's dad, have you?"

"Nope," I said.

"But you know some things about Sean's father?"

I decided to lie. He might not hold back about Sean's father if he thought I knew stuff about him. "No doubt," I said. "Me and Sean tight."

"Cool," Davon said. "Cool. When I first got to Clinton, I met Sean's pops and he looked out for me. Now I'm out, and me and him speak on the regular."

Above Ms. Feeney's desk was our class picture, blown up poster-style. Davon pointed at it and put his finger right on Sean's face. "This is Sean, right?"

"Yep," I said.

"Monday I was in this room meeting with your teacher," Davon said. "We were at this desk planning today's Advisory and I looked up and this picture almost made my jaw hit the floor. Sean's face popped out at me immediately. We met a few weeks back when we were both visiting his dad in Clinton. I told Ms. Feeney, 'This is Sean, right?' She bugged out. Her eyes went wide. I told her how I knew him. That's when she told me Sean had just fought in here. She said he threw the first punch. True?"

I stuffed my hands in my hoodie's pockets. I shrugged. "I don't know."

"Why'd you want me to speak with me, little man?"

"I'm worried about Sean," I said.

"Me too," he said. "Ms. Feeney says she sees Sean put kids down all the time. Now he's stepping it up to another level. Fistfighting. She asked me to see if Sean's dad knows. I'll see about Sean's pops, but let me ask you something."

"Yeah?"

"You tried speaking to Sean? The way you talking with me? To stop his stupidness?"

I wasn't sure, but Davon's voice sounded how Sean's moms' did when she told me I should've tried harder to keep Sean out of trouble. Jackie putting that on me back then made me feel guilty, and Davon putting this on me now made me feel bad again. I got tight because I wished I could do something, but Sean wasn't listening to me. I wanted to stay quiet but I decided to tell Davon that.

"I tried," I said, "but he's been acting mad different. I don't think he'll listen to me."

"You should try speaking to him again," Davon continued. "I don't know much about Sean's relationship with his pops. I do know that when I saw them during that visit, Sean sat as far from his dad as he could. The whole time. Once in a while, Sean's father gave him a compliment, but Sean twisted his lips like 'Whatever.'

"Sean kept shooting stank looks at him too. Yo, your boy got hostility against his old man. Maybe it was just that visit but they didn't seem close. So I'll speak with Sean's pops but you talking to Sean might have more of an impact.

"When I was your age, I listened to my boys more than my parents. Sean's heading the wrong way. Can you kick it with him? Maybe turn him around?"

I checked on Davon's friends. They were near the windows talking. Ms. Feeney was at her file cabinet flicking through folders. "Yeah," I told him. "I'll try talking with Sean."

"Cool, little man." Davon smiled.

At the same time we both put our hands out for a goodbye pound.

"Merry belated Christmas," he said.

"Thanks," I said. "Happy late New Year's too."

I stared back at Ms. Feeney. She was busy at her file cabinet so I nodded peace to Davon and bounced.

Who Knew?

SO SEAN'S FATHER'S IN JAIL. Sean must've visited him those Saturdays. Part of me wanted to run and tell Vanessa and Kyle Sean's secret and what had happened between me and that jail guy in Advisory. But part of me felt like I needed to keep Sean's secret for maybe the same reasons he kept this thing with his dad a secret in the first place. For the same reasons that me and a lot of kids from our projects and school stayed quiet or lied about our fathers.

Maybe like us he was too embarrassed to admit he didn't have the perfect family that be on almost every TV channel. I knew I was ashamed my father wasn't around, and my dad wasn't even in prison.

I wondered if Sean's moms told him not to put his family business about his dad in the street.

Or maybe Sean made up stuff about where his dad was because it hurt to be real about whatever got his dad locked up.

I knew one thing for sure. If our neighborhood and school knew Sean had a locked-up dad, that would've made him like everyone else with deadbeat dads. He couldn't be king of the hill no more.

But even after all my thinking, I still was mad at the fact that he had lied to me.

Anyway, I couldn't tell Vanessa and Kyle about Sean right now if I wanted to. Vanessa's and Kyle's parents pulled them from school early. Vanessa left school at two o'clock with her mom to go to a dentist appointment in Williamsburg. I already knew Kyle's father had gotten him from school at one thirty so they could visit Kyle's grandparents on Long Island.

I had finally learned Sean's secret. Now, was sharing it with Vanessa and Kyle the right thing to do? Maybe I should just do what that giant told me. Speak to Sean. My thoughts felt tied up in my head. Maybe I needed to write in my rhymebook. It was home, so I rushed there.

My mother was in the bathroom hanging wet clothes to dry when I got home.

"Ma," I said. "Can we talk?"

She slung my last wet T-shirt onto a hanger. "Sure. What's up?" She looked nervous and probably thought something bad had happened with me. She wore the same outfit she always did when she did laundry. Her extra-large green T-shirt that said "Brooklyn" in white script, black sweatpants, and white tube socks. Her hair was pulled back in a bun.

"Nothing's wrong with me," I said.

"Good. You got me worried."

"You know how Ms. Feeney invites guest speakers for Advisory?" I said. "Today we met guys from jail."

"Really?" Ma sounded impressed. "What you learn?"

"One guy knows Sean's father. From jail."

"Didn't Sean say his dad lives in PR?" Ma said, squinting like she didn't understand and was looking for me to repeat myself.

"Sean lied," I said. "His dad's really been in jail. He's there now. Him and his mom probably went there that time we saw them."

Ma nodded.

"What I don't get," I said, "is where that Puerto Rican stuff on Sean's dresser came from."

"What stuff?"

"Sean says those key chains, toys, and stuff on his dresser are from his father, in Puerto Rico."

"Justin," Ma said. "Wake up. Half of Sean's family is from PR. Maybe they send him stuff and he just says it's from his dad. You know, to front so people won't think his father's locked up."

"You surprised Sean's dad's in jail?"

"No," Ma said. "Something didn't make sense about his story. His father was supposed to be in Puerto Rico but still with Jackie? And he loved Sean? Then why didn't he once visit Sean in Red Hook? What free man, who's cool with both his wife and son, lives two, three hours from here and can't visit them?"

"True."

"Him being locked up might also explain why Jackie stays on a hi-and-bye basis with me. You and Sean are best friends, but she never got close with me. Isn't that strange? She kept her distance to keep the business with Sean's dad private. So no, it doesn't surprise me Sean's dad's in jail. Looking back, now it makes sense."

"Sean's father is in jail," I said again, loud. I checked to see if Ma thought I was bugging for repeating myself, but she just looked sorry for me.

"All this time," I said, "Sean's been dissing kids for having deadbeat dads. It's Sean who has the deadbeat dad."

"That's how it is," Ma said. "If someone feels bad

about something, he points it out in other people. When I was young, I hated my teeth, so I teased kids about their teeth. While everybody was focused on those kids, nobody was focused on me."

"But what about Sean getting new games and clothes?" I asked. "Sean's mom is a cashier at IKEA. And his dad's locked up. They don't own a house and land in PR like Sean said. His mom can't afford all his new stuff. Where does his extra cash come from? I thought his dad mailed him that money from PR."

"Maybe she has other family helping her out," Ma said. "They could be throwing money her way on the side. That could explain Sean's games, cash, and clothes."

"Ma, Sean's a fake friend! All his lies. The first lie: his pops is in PR. His second lie: the stuff on his dresser was from his dad, from Puerto Rico. His father didn't send that. He lied to me and said he went to Jersey and Philly this year, but he didn't. He's been a fake friend."

"Stop acting silly, Justin," Ma said. "Sean's not a fake friend. He lied about his father. But can you trust Sean with other stuff? If you got into a fight, would Sean jump in?"

"Yeah."

"When I didn't get my check and you wanted to go paintballing with Sean, what happened?"

"Sean paid my way. And he didn't ask me for the money back."

I thought about me and Sean and the Grey House. He had chances but he had never once told anyone I had climbed the Grey House. Yeah, I could trust Sean with stuff. Maybe Sean was a real friend. But how could a real friend be honest with you about one thing and lie to you about another thing?

"Justin, do you think I know everything about my friends?" Ma asked.

I thought she did.

"My friends and I sometimes keep things from each other," Ma said. "But we have each other's backs where it matters. You don't know why Sean lied. Maybe he's ashamed his dad's in jail. Maybe Jackie told him to lie about where his father was. We don't know. But you can't fault Sean for hiding something like that. If your dad was in jail, would you tell other kids?"

I knew my answer. No, I wouldn't tell. And I probably would lie too about where my dad was. Ma reached out and stroked my forehead. I half smiled at her and she pinched my cheek.

"Don't think Sean's not your best friend because he didn't tell you about his father. He probably was just protecting himself. Maybe he thought you'd joke on his dad."

"I wonder," I said, "if Sean felt that if his own father could hurt him by going to jail and leaving him to survive alone, then maybe us, his closest friends, who aren't even his blood, could hurt him worse than his dad did."

"That's probably part of it," Ma said.

I thought about how Ma talks about boys in the projects being hard. Maybe Sean kept the truth in because he was so used to pretending nothing was wrong with him. Ma hated it when I hid things from my guy friends. Maybe this was why.

"You mind if I go to my room?" I asked Ma.

"Go ahead, sweetie."

I lay back on my bed thinking about Sean.

Maybe Sean's a fake friend, I thought. Maybe he's not and I should forgive him.

I kept going over the situation again and again like a dog chasing its tail. I couldn't decide if Sean was a fake friend or worth forgiving. I also couldn't keep my eyes open anymore.

I fell into a deep sleep and had a wild dream.

My mom knocked on my door. "Your dad's here to see you," she said.

For a second, I didn't believe I heard her right. "What?" I asked.

"Your father," she said, "is here." A man's

voice grunted and I knew it was him. It was as if my body took over. I couldn't think and, right then, every bad feeling I had for my pops disappeared. I flew out of bed with the quickness and tried turning my doorknob, but it wouldn't twist. "I can't open the door!" I yelled. "Open it for me!"

"Just turn the knob," Ma said.

I tried again, using all the strength I had. "Ma! It's stuck!" I shouted, kicking the door. "Open it!"

"Well," I heard my father's voice say, "it's his fault if he doesn't see me. I'm leaving."

"Dad." I started crying. "It's not my fault. Stay." Boogers and tears poured into my mouth and I snorted. "Don't leave! It's not my fault!"

"Bye," my father said to my mother. "I won't be back."

The door to our apartment slammed and Ma locked it.

I got so mad that I grabbed my computer and slammed it into pieces on the floor. I wanted to see him more than anything. Whatever I could touch, I threw and broke. I grabbed my baseball bat and swung every-where. Bits of broken toys, shattered plastic from CD cases, and other things flew all over. Then out of nowhere, a voice asked me, "That was your pops? It's good you didn't see him. He's not who you think he is."

The voice came from my full-length mirror. I slowly walked over to it. Who I saw bugged me out.

Sean. He was my reflection. I slowly lifted my hand. In the same way he did too. He made every move I did. I was Sean. He was me.

I stepped back from the mirror. "W-what?" I fake-stuttered to throw him off, but my Sean reflection spoke exactly like me. "Y-you i-in th-there?" we both said.

"What you expect?" Sean laughed. "You and me are the same. They don't want us."

I got so mad at what he said I swung my bat at the mirror and shouted curses. No matter how many pieces I broke the mirror into, Sean was in every reflection.

Soon Sean's voice echoed from each shattered piece. "You me! I'm you! You me! I'm you!" The sound of a hundred Seans filled the room. In some reflections Sean was crying, and in others he was laughing or serious.

I picked up one piece and it reflected Sean's face melting and looking more like me.

His eyes and nose turned into my eyes and nose. Soon he had my ears and forehead. It scared me and I threw the glass down.

The nightmare gave me a bad headache, but it also made me see things differently. Things I hadn't seen before.

Fake Friend or What?

THE NEXT DAY while watching Saturday morning cartoons, I thought about Vanessa and Kyle.

Holding back from them didn't feel right. For different reasons.

Vanessa had gone to Sean's place and took his rhymebook.

I owed Kyle too. When I confronted Sean in the gym, Kyle wasn't normal chill Kyle. He stepped up. Called Sean out about his secret Saturdays.

Yeah, right now, I was the one with all of Sean's information. But along the way, we three had worked to get it.

You need to tell them, I thought.

I flicked my cell open and dialed Kyle's number.

"Hello?" he answered.

"Let's three-way with Vanessa," I said. "It's about Sean."

When Vanessa picked up, I said, "I need you both to meet me at my place later. I found out the missing pieces about Sean."

When they showed up, I brought them to my room, shut the door, and told them everything.

"Sean's such a liar!" Vanessa said.

"For real!" Kyle said.

They reacted the same way I had.

I told them, "Try to think of Sean lying this way. He probably felt his dad hurt him by getting locked up. Maybe he feels if his own family could hurt him, then we could hurt him too. We aren't even his blood." Vanessa and Kyle didn't say anything. I wanted them to see too that maybe Sean wasn't so grimy for lying.

After a few more seconds of quiet, Vanessa said, "Yeah. I can see what you mean."

"Me too," Kyle said. "Kind of. I know one thing: I wouldn't want people knowing my dad was in jail."

"That's why we shouldn't tell Sean we know he's sneaking to see his father," I said.

Kyle's eyes were confused, but he nodded.

"Let's just keep this to ourselves," Vanessa said. "We three know. If Sean finds out we know, we'll handle it. But for now, let's keep it quiet. You were right, though, Justin. Sean bugged out the same time he started seeing his pops in prison."

"Yep," I said.

"Seeing his dad locked up was probably too much for him," Kyle said.

"Yeah," I said. "In his raps he says he doesn't even want to go and his mom drags him there. He's probably wilding out because he wants her to stop it but he doesn't want to tell her."

"If going to jail is messing Sean up, his mother needs to stop taking him there for real," Vanessa said. "She thinks because Sean's a boy, he needs to see his father, but Sean'll get left back if he keeps acting up in school."

"So we just keep hanging out with Sean and act normal?" Kyle asked.

Vanessa looked at Kyle. "Yeah."

"For real, though," Kyle said, "I don't know if I can go back to normal with him. I understand why he might've lied to us, but knowing he's a liar will make me feel weird around him. He's a fake friend."

"So what?" Vanessa said. "You going to stop hanging with him?" She turned to me. "Justin, you think Sean's a fake friend too?"

Fake friend. I thought back to the time I called Vanessa a fake friend in the stadium for lying about

173

liking Sean. I even told her she didn't understand what friendship meant. But from how Vanessa acted with this whole Sean thing, she knew a lot about friendship. She had Sean's back from the get-go. And it wasn't because she had a crush on him. She was a real friend.

"Kyle," I said, "Sean has enough with his father being in jail. I feel you that Sean's a liar. But at the same time, I'm thinking he doesn't need us, his tightest friends, acting ill with him."

"Yeah," Vanessa agreed. "Like Justin said, all Sean has is his front and us. He doesn't need us exposing him and switching up."

Kyle pushed his glasses up his nose and shook his head. He heard us but needed more convincing. "Sean has had our backs since fourth grade," I said. "Now that he's slipping, we should have his. Being friends isn't knowing everything about each other." It made me feel good saying that, but I knew what Kyle was feeling. It would be weird knowing Sean was smiling in our faces but lying to us. In the end, we decided the best way to be his friend was to pretend we didn't know Sean's secret. I felt guilty inside. Vanessa and Kyle probably felt as grimy as me but I didn't ask them. We were wrong for stealing Sean's rhymebook. We needed to know what was up with him and we found out in a sneaky way. Yeah, he lied to us about his secret but we lied to learn his secret. All these lies on top of lies and now more pretending made me feel like I was buried under a mountain of crap and wanted to climb out.

How It Is

BY THE MIDDLE OF JANUARY, Sean was back. It felt like forever since he'd been in school. But he seemed like his old self. He came to school on time and he didn't miss a day.

He hung out with us on the regular. I stopped seeing him be around his cousin and his eighth-grade crew. He even handed in crisp work.

And something new was up with him. He didn't dis kids.

He even went back to freestyling with me, which was maybe his way of saying we were back to normal with each other. One day after school me and him were at the cab station arcade on Crazy Corner. We stood side by side, aiming our video-game guns at the game screen while we blasted zombies. He freestyled first:

I got caught up for a minute and didn't like the aftermath.
Being suspended, getting punished. That crap was wack.
I spent a lot of time thinking, and from now on I'm chillin'.

While shooting body parts off people climbing out of graves, I rhymed back:

Ayo, we here shooting deadheads and life seems cool.
Things are back to normal. You doing good in school.
You had me, Kyle, and Vanessa worried for a minute but you back on track.
You fistfighting Manny was bugged, though.
We didn't know how to react.

He didn't respond for a second because we entered the next level of the game and mad zombies jumped out an abandoned building and bum-rushed us. Me and him fired until we got rid of everyone and the game said our guns were empty. While we waited for our weapons to reload and for more zombies to show, Sean finished his rap.

You want to hear something funny?
Keep this between you and me.
I felt a bit grimy about beating up Manny.
Yeah, he shows no respect so he should expect to get checked.
But since when did I fight with my hands? That was bugged.
When that happened, I knew I was switching up.
The old me is back. The one who knows how to act.

With his eyes on the game Sean couldn't see me, but I smiled. I was happy to hear him say my best friend was back. What if he goes on another secret trip and doesn't tell you? I thought. Will he be my best friend then? I decided not to think about it. I was just amped that we back to being cool.

Weeks passed and things stayed normal with Sean.

Me, Kyle, and him did our sleepovers. If Sean didn't do them, on Friday, me and Kyle stayed up late at my place to see if Sean and his mom snuck to go upstate. They didn't. Maybe Jackie stopped taking Sean there because she figured out him going to prison was messing up his head and sending him in the wrong direction. If so, Sean's mom was smart.

Two months later, in March, me, Vanessa, Kyle, and Sean were in school at lunch.

"Fight him at three. Don't be like Stupid Sean and get suspended for fighting." This seventh grader, Tyler, dissed him loud enough for our whole table to hear.

"You just called me stupid?" Sean put his sandwich down and turned to Tyler.

"Yeah," Tyler said. "You know you were stupid for fighting in school."

For a long time now nobody had bothered Sean. And Sean hadn't bothered anyone. Now Tyler was starting with him. He probably thought Sean was soft because Sean had stopped dissing on kids.

Sean looked at me. At Vanessa. At Kyle. For the first time, I saw someone dis Sean and Sean didn't have that "fight back" fire in his eye. Sean shook his head at Tyler and bit into his sandwich.

"You letting Tyler dis on you?" some girl asked Sean.

Sean paid her no mind. He kept chewing.

"Dang, Sean," some boy shouted. "You booty."

Tyler wouldn't stop either. "Let Sean eat, because he knows I'll dis him so hard, he'll cry," he said to everybody.

"Ohhh!" some kids at our table said.

Sean's nostrils flared.

Ignore them, Sean, I thought. I wish I had that superpower to control people's minds. I would've used it. To hypnotize Sean into forgetting about Tyler and everybody here beasting. After, I'd make Tyler dive into a garbage can as tall as us. Come out with tomato sauce and spaghetti noodles dripping from his head. But that was make-believe. In reality, I knew Sean couldn't just stay dissed in front of a crowd. And I couldn't make Tyler and these kids relax.

Out here the rule was "Dis or get dissed on." The best disser was king of the hill. Kids knew that was Sean.

Sean finally looked up. Maybe he was annoyed at everybody laughing at him. His eyes were different. He winked at me like he did before he threw his one-two knockout combo of disses. He smiled at Tyler as if Tyler was his dessert.

"With your wino father, you shouldn't dis on me," Sean said.

The whole lunch table exploded with kids laughing. Tyler squinted at Sean. Tyler knew he couldn't say anything. Sean was telling the truth. Everyone knew Tyler's father was the drunk, homeless, toothless man named Peter who wandered Red Hook Projects, sleeping on benches, begging kids for money, and collecting cans.

Sean paused.

Mad kids were watching and waiting for him to keep dissing Tyler.

Sean's doing like my mother said, I thought. He's focused everybody on laughing at another kid's father and no one is even looking at Sean. So no one thinks Sean might be the one with the deadbeat dad.

"Son, just the other day," Sean said, "I was going in the supermarket and I had to step over your pops because he was laid out, drunk, on the floor, blocking my entrance."

"Ooooo!" kids said.

Tyler stood up like maybe he wanted to fight Sean.

"Don't even think about coming over here to fight," Sean said. "That girl, Melly, busted your lip last month, so you know I'll knock you out. Just like I did to Manny. I'll wipe your pimply face on this floor and wax it with your zit juice." Kids looked at Tyler and waited for him to say or do something, but Tyler was stuck on stupid for a second. He just sat there. Maybe wondering what to do next. He finally decided to leave.

Everybody at the tabled laughed at Tyler for bouncing.

"Punk," one kid yelled at Tyler's back. Tyler kept going.

"Sucker," a girl screamed.

Kids started giving Sean props and he smiled big at them. They gave him pounds. Patted him on the back. Including Vanessa and Kyle. Everyone except me.

Sean finally leaned over to me for a pound, saying, "I got that one."

"You got it," I said, putting my fist out to him, but I didn't mean it.

We were back to old times. Sean showed he could beat up a kid with his words. He grinned at me like I should want to be him. A few months ago, I did. Except things were different now.

Now, I was realizing stuff.

Sean being quick with a dis used to mean he was The Man, but not anymore.

Sean went from dissing kids to bullying kids to putting his hands on them. I used to think his mom's advice was hot. "Beat up kids with words so other kids get scared and don't mess with you." Yeah, dissing stopped kids from bothering you, but it was bad in a way too. Those jail guys had talked in Advisory about traps. Maybe following the rule "Dis or get dissed on" was a trap too. Because dissing trapped Sean into being mean. It trapped him into fronting too. Made him a liar. He hid things about himself from everybody. Even from me. His tightest friend.

I couldn't stand to sit there, watching kids treat Sean like he and everything was perfect. I got up and left.

How I Wish It Was

EVEN THOUGH THINGS HAD BEEN BACK TO NORMAL with Sean for months, my mind was still stuck on loop. Sometimes, I felt cool with him. Other times, I didn't know how to feel. Like right now.

On my dresser was a picture of me and him smiling at an amusement park. I flung the book I was reading at that picture. The book knocked the frame flat.

I turned on my TV, and the first channel had this new talk show called *Debra*. The guest was a man who looked like a supersized, diesel Sean. Half of me wanted to switch the channel, but another part of me was freaked out by how much that man really looked like Sean. It was bugged, as if I were seeing the real Sean grown up in some way.

On a screen behind the man and the host, Debra, were a few photos of the guy playing NFL football. He was a famous athlete, but I didn't know him because I didn't watch football. Vanessa, Kyle, and Sean weren't into football either.

In one picture, the man wasn't in his football uniform. He wore a suit and stood next to the president. They were both smiling and had their hands on the same award. Maybe the president gave him that? Bigger than that picture was an even larger photo of a book with this man's face on it. He must've written it. It was called *How Can We Make Being a Man Mean More?*

The camera showed two ladies standing in the audience. One woman had Hershey-brown skin and a cute face, with her hair in tiny, curly dreadlock twists. She rocked a pink, tight turtleneck. The other lady was White and had on a black T-shirt. She must've worked for the show, because she handed the Black lady a microphone.

"Thank you. Hi. First off, I love you, Debra. I'm a big fan." To the man, she said, "My question is about your fraternity. You're saying in college you were with men in your fraternity 24/7, yet you still feel you didn't know the real them? And they didn't know the real you?"

On the screen behind the man and Debra now

was a photo of the man and about twelve other guys dressed in tuxedos. They all were standing shoulder to shoulder and had their arms around each other, hugging tightly. They were smiling big at whoever was taking that photo. Black men. Latino. Asian. Two White guys.

Debra pointed at the picture. "Is that your fraternity?"

From the picture, I guessed that a fraternity meant his group of homeboys in college.

"Yeah."

"Nice shot of you," Debra said.

He winked at her. "Thank you."

He nodded to the lady in the audience and said, "Yes, the guys and me in that picture call ourselves brothers, but in many ways, we were and are strangers. We hid stuff from each other. We still do. For example, issues with my father. Take alcoholism. It runs in my family. I knew for sure that some of my closest boys had an alcoholic parent too. But we never talked about that. For a few reasons. Fear of looking weak or soft. Also, us not knowing how to handle those conversations. Whatever felt awkward to discuss, we kept inside."

"Why do you think so many men are that way?" the lady said.

Debra made a curious face and asked her, "What way?"

"All macho."

He laughed. "Let me ask you a question. How many times have you seen a boy make this 'muscle man' pose for a picture?" He flexed his biceps.

The lady said, "A lot."

"Me too," Debra said. "We all have, right?"

Almost everyone in the audience agreed.

"You see that?" the man said. "We all come from different places yet we know the same thing. Boys think it's cool to look strong. Why? Because before boys can walk, they're programmed with messages to be hard. They follow that script and grow into men who act as she said—hard and macho."

"Where do boys get the message 'Be hard' from?" Debra asked.

"Sports, movies, music. Our families, schools. The list goes on."

"And you think tough isn't the way to go?" Debra asked. "I mean, some women like a tough man. It makes them feel protected."

"True. There are some places and times guys need to show toughness. Not everywhere and all the time, though. We need to teach boys when to turn that hardness off and show other sides. Otherwise, boys act tough in places they don't need to. Then they grow into men who act that way."

"How can a guy change?" Debra asked him. "Be more multidimensional?"

"For me, I first had to see if I was a stereotype of a man. Next, I had to stop being that stereotype and act differently. It's hard. When I changed, some of my friends acted weird. Some made jokes. But others were true friends. I was real with them and they were real right back. Meaning they didn't put me down and they helped me work through my issues."

"This is an important topic," Debra said. "Why is it close to your heart?"

"One day, I hope to have a son. I want him to know from young that wearing a front and acting tough isn't the way to be all the time. I'm not saying to boys, 'Tell everybody your issues.' I'm saying this: 'Don't hide. Don't hide yourself behind one way of acting, and don't hide your problems from people you think you can trust.'

"I did that and it limited me in my friendships. Many boys stay hush about their issues and their issues don't get addressed. That can mess them up in their adult lives. We need to stop that."

The audience clapped.

Seeing this man made me think about when me and Sean become adults. I wondered if the wack things about our lives from right now would mess us up for good. Like when Sean became twenty-five years old, would he still be lying about his father? Would both me and him be men and still be fronting and acting hard? Putting our real thoughts in raps in notebooks but afraid to be real with each other? Scared to be honest with other grown guys? It wasn't just me and Sean. It was this football player and his friends too. And most boys out here in Red Hook and school tried to act hard. If you didn't, you got punked.

I wondered if I'd be a dad someday. When I was grown, if I had a son, I'd teach him he didn't need to follow the stupid rule of "Dis or get dissed on." Me and Sean wore an armor all the time, how Ma said. Me and Sean kept things from each other, and that made us into liars with people we're supposed to be close to. I'd raise my son different. No lies between him and his friends.

I hated Sean's father. That deadbeat. Sean was so ashamed of him that he lied about his family just to seem normal. I hated my deadbeat dad too. They should just stop acting like big kids and see that their being gone so much, hanging out all the time, and leaving their families messed their kids up. I was pissed at my mom's brother for going to jail. I lied all the time about where he was at and I couldn't stand it.

Most kids out here lied. But for what? The next kid had something wrong with their family too.

And Ms. Feeney tried to make the way Sean was all his fault. As if he enjoyed messing with kids. But our school and neighborhood had traps the way that prison dude in Advisory said. Sean just fell into traps at times. When Manny and Sean beefed, it was Manny who started it. Manny put that trap out there. Plus, those times in the cafeteria, where Sean clowned those kids, Sean didn't pick on them. Those kids tried getting names for themselves, and they dissed on Sean first. He defended himself and fell into another trap.

And what about the other kids at the lunch table? They were waiting and pushing Sean to dis on kids. Like in Ms. Feeney's class, when Sean and Manny fought, mad kids yelled, "Fight! Fight! Fight!" They weren't screaming, "Stop! Stop! Stop!" And when Sean did dis or fight, kids gave him props for being good at it. That's another trap too.

Out here it's "Fight, fight, fight." If you can, you're The Man. Even Sean's mother told him, "Be the one kids are scared of because if they are, they'll leave you alone." Ms. Feeney was stupid for blaming just Sean. She should point fingers at everybody else too.

The man who looked like Sean was still on the TV. I tried to imagine he was the real Sean, just grown up, free from all the drama the kid Sean grew up with. The show cut to a commercial. I grabbed the remote and zapped the TV off.

For some reason, the *Debra* show reminded me of this line from Black Bald, my favorite rapper.

Black's rhyme went:

"By nine, I was addicted to street life.

As a boy, that's when the kid in me died.

Even when I was my truest, I was a fake, just a lie.

Doing grimy things all the time to get a high, to get by."

Have I ever been grimy with Sean? I thought. The answer came fast. Nope. I never lied to Sean. I started thinking about secrets I should've kept but had told him throughout our friendship.

Like when I was younger and my high school cousin Carl disappeared. He came back a year later with this huge scar on his face like somebody had sliced him. One day, Sean pointed it out and told me, "Dudes get cut like that in jail. Where'd Carl go when he left?" I knew for a fact I'd told Sean Carl was in jail. Oh! No, I didn't. I didn't want him or anyone knowing I had cousins in jail. I lied to Sean. I told him Carl was in the army.

Nah. What about that time my grown cousin Victor decided he was gay? He showed up on our block dressed like a woman, asking people to call him Vicky. Me and Sean were on the benches watching Vicky switch his skinny butt all up and down our block. Snapping his fingers and stuff.

"Son! Isn't that gay dude your cousin?" Sean asked me.

I manned up and told him, "Yes."

Oh dip! No, I didn't. I was too embarrassed I had a gay cousin. That's another time I lied to Sean. I told him some doodoo about Vicky not being blood-related to me.

But what about the biggest secret of mine? Why my dad left. I knew I'd told Sean the whole story with that. Nope. I hadn't. I didn't like that my father cheated on my mother and didn't tell him that part. All I told him was where my father went and that me and my pops didn't talk anymore.

And when me, my moms, and Sean were up on Fulton Street and Ma bought groceries and paid for it with her welfare card, Sean caught that and whispered to me, "Son, you on welfare?" I lied and said my moms had borrowed her friend Maggie's card. I knew Sean knew I was on welfare, especially after I saw what he wrote in his rhymebook. But I never told him the truth.

My mind suddenly turned to Advisory when the gang guy asked us to raise our hands if we didn't come from a normal family. I didn't blame kids for not announcing that, because they'd get dissed on later for it, but I hated on Sean because he didn't tell me, Vanessa, and Kyle he had a messed-up family.

Man. Sean had betrayed me, but I had betrayed him too.

I remembered the rest of Black Bald's rap:

"Real friends help you get through. Your boys are just mirror images of you."

I remembered that nightmare I'd had. I was the same as Sean.

I went to the top drawer of my dresser. Under my socks was my half of the piece of metal from the Grey House. I ran my fingers over its sharp edges where Sean had broken it in two. He still had his half. I picked up the picture I had knocked down. I was done with going back and forth in my head about Sean. I wanted us to be tight again. Period.

Back at the Grey House, I thought I knew everything about friendship. It was about trust. But right now, friendship meant I wished Sean would put himself out there with me. Let me know the real him. All parts of him. I remembered something my mother used to say when I was in elementary school. "You have to be the type of friend you want." Thinking that made me realize I wasn't the type of friend I wanted Sean to be to me.

I was afraid to tell him stuff because I thought he'd look down on me. But I hated on him for being scared to tell me things.

I lied to him at times, but I wanted him to be real all the time with me.

If you want a real friend, I thought, you have to be a real friend. Suddenly I had an idea of what to do. I went and got my rhymebook out of my top drawer, then checked the digital clock on my dresser. 7:05. Not too late. I could still call Sean to chill. Man up and tell him things I'd kept from him. Maybe read him some of my raps with the truth about my father and my cousins Carl and Vicky. I knew I had written verses on them at the time.

Maybe tell Sean how I felt when he punked me and didn't accept the homework I'd copied for him. Maybe him seeing more parts of me would get him open. Then he'd share more parts of him, like the truth about his dad.

I went to my desk and pulled my cell out of its charger. I was scared but I dialed Sean's cell anyway. It rang twice.

"Hello?"

"It's me," I said. I swallowed, nervous. "Can you come downstairs?"

"Yeah. What up?" he said all calm.

My heart started beating fast and hard. "I have some stuff I need to get off my chest," I said.

Sean didn't answer. Was he thinking he had some things he wanted to get off his chest with me? Or was he changing his mind about coming down? Me and him needed to talk. If he backed out now, I'd have to hype myself up all over again to tell him this stuff.

"Yeah," Sean said, then paused. "I'll be down there in one minute."

I got happy. All of a sudden, I remembered my mother saying, "Boys and men out here think they can't ever be sensitive because that's considered soft or gay. And if the next guy shows some gentle emotion, they say he's soft or gay." What would Sean think when he was down here and I began telling him things? Would he see me as gay or soft for being raw with him? Whatever, I thought. Time to man up.

ACKNOWLEDGMENTS

This book happened thanks to the right people at the right time.

First, thank you to Charlotte Sheedy and Stacey Barney for an amazing ride. Charlotte, you knew which road to take. Stacey, you had the road map to drive my first book to the finish line.

I'm forever grateful to E. R. Frank. E.R., you're real and our planet is better because of you. I deeply appreciate Mwezi Pugh for being one of my first readers. Your students are lucky to have you.

I can't thank my mother enough. Ma, you sacrificed so I had an excellent childhood, bright future, and wonderful "right now." Your love of reading and writing made me love reading and writing. You set high goals for me while knocking down low expectations others had for me. You taught me that my free mind mixed with motivation can do the impossible.

To my mother's mother, Milagros, you were true to your name; and a miracle for me. You made space for my childhood drawings, and that grew into my painting pictures with words.

A big shout-out to my sisters, nieces, and nephews for your realness and support. Thanks also to my in-laws for showing me that family is more than who you're born with.

For my wife and daughter, I love you. To my wife, you've helped keep alive the fire that my mother lit in my heart and fanned it to grow. To my daughter, you're incredible—a little me plus more. You both are part of the everyday net that catches me, comforts me, and boosts me to new and greater heights.

Thank you to my Red Hook Community and my extended Red Hook family. Thanks to all my supporters from P.S. 15, J.H.S. 142, M.S. 88, Midwood High School, and Vassar College.

Justin and Sean's Playlist

(Message from Justin and Sean: Whatever newest, hottest songs come out, we listen to. This mix of hits makes us do different things. After playing these songs, our problems don't feel so big: we feel hyped to write our raps, freestyle, and more.)

Eminem – "Beautiful"

B.o.B. with Hayley Williams – "Airplanes"

Tinie Tempah with Eric Turner – "Written in the Stars"

T.I. with Rihanna – "Live Your Life"

Lupe Fiasco - "The Show Goes On"

Nas – "I Can"

Dilated Peoples with Kanye West – "This Way"

Talib Kweli – "Just To Get By"

T.I. with Justin Timberlake – "Dead and Gone"

Tupac – "Dear Mama"

Mary J. Blige – "No More Drama"

Diddy with Skylar Grey – "I'm Coming Home"

Discussion Guide

1. In the stadium, Sean pressures Justin to do a dare that Justin feels uncomfortable doing. What is it about the Grey House that makes Sean and Justin want to trespass and go into it? If you were Justin, how would you have responded to Sean pressuring you to go into the Grey House?

2. Why does Justin want to know where Sean secretly goes?

3. Since both Sean and Justin are being raised only by their mothers, they have a lot they can talk about. So what might be some reasons both boys never talk about their fathers?

4. New Year's Eve and Halloween make people act in certain ways in Justin's neighborhood. How does Justin feel about his neighborhood on these holidays? Why does Justin say, "My mother always was a nervous wreck on Halloween"(p. 62)? Support your answer with details from the book.

5. Justin says that he is one part Kyle and one part Sean. Think of two persons your age who

you admire. If you could have one quality from each of them, what quality would you pick?

6. Toward the end of the book, Justin realizes Vanessa knows something about friendship that Justin did not know. What does Justin feel Vanessa knows about friendship? What makes a person a good friend?

7. Principal Negron says a fistfight is just one step on a staircase of violence. What does he feel is one of the first steps leading up to a fistfight? Do you agree? Explain.

8. Why does Sean keep his secret from Justin? If you were Sean, what would you have done?

9. To people who do not know him, Sean might be a "bad kid." Do you think Sean is a "bad kid"? Why or why not?

10. Justin has to make a big decision at the end of *Secret Saturdays*. What do you think about his decision?